A Death In Passing

Karen L. Abrahamson

A NEW MYSTERY

Yamin waited, listening for the vicious monkeys to return or for a human to enter the golden cloth awning. Gradually his breathing slowed and his fear subsided. Escaping the monkeys had been almost fun. He wasn't sure whether he would do it again, but he might.

He dusted off his blue pantaloons.

It was strange that the awning interior was so silent. He inspected the effigy—this Min Mahagiri had a particularly pudgy rear—something that the true Min Mahagiri wouldn't like given the great nat's vanity. The elephant was pitiably small, too—and he'd always heard that elephants were incredibly tall. Disappointing, really.

He stepped out from behind the effigy and looked out into the covered area under the awning. The yellow cloth turned the grass golden. The musical instruments were a clutter on the ground, the three-foot-tall bamboo slats around the gong circle masking what lay behind the instruments under the awning.

Yamin froze. Stretched out on the ground on his back as if he were sleeping lay the nat wife. The satiny woman's shirt with its flouncy ruffled bottom gave his identity away. So did the rouge on the pale face above the neck that so clearly had an Adam's apple. Eyes, black as tree shadows, looked up at the awning and Yamin cringed back, praying not to be seen.

Still, the nat wife didn't move. Yamin stepped closer and realized his feet were sinking into wet grass. Blood pooled around the base of the nat effigy and around Yamin's puppet-sized toes.

Fantasy and Mystery by Karen L. Abrahamson

Mystery (Writing as K.L. Abrahamson)
Through Dark Water

Fantasy Mystery
Aung and Yamin Series
Death By Effigy (Guardbridge Books)
A Death in Passing
Death In Umber

The Cartographer Universe
(in chronological order)
The Warden of Power
Impossible
The Cartographer's Daughter
The American Geological Survey Series:
Afterburn
Aftershock
Aftermath
Afterimage
Terra Incognita
Terra Infirma
Terra Nueva

Other Fantasy Novels
Ice Dragon
Emberstone
Mutable Things
The Crystal Courtesan

A Death

In

Passing

Chapter 1

During the month of Nayon in the heart of Burma, when the moon is full and the many springs and streams of Mount Popa run full and laughing through the deep green jungles with the water of the little rains, the people of Bagan and from the villages at the foot of the great mountain leave their homes and bring their offerings: coconut, betel, bananas, and rice to the nats of the mountain.

The long road up the mountain slope fills with laughter and a spirit of celebration, and among the people travel the nat dancers, those who are wives to the great spirits.

While some nat dancers are women, many are men and *pnadaka*—florid in their presentation as they flourish their artful fingers in dancers' poses. They wear silken blouses and scarves twined in their long hair like women. Through them, and the nats who possess them, the people of the villages give thanks to the spirits to gain luck, health, and prosperity.

Or risk the ills of the nats for the next year.

In the shade of a thicket of towering bamboo, Aung Aung the puppet singer stretched out his back after the long climb up the mountainside and tried once more to rid himself of the sense of doom that had dogged him on his journey. Perhaps it was only the many clouds floating across the sky that threatened the little rains, but Aung did not think so. His worry dwelt deep near his heart, for the world was changing.

On the moist earth near a jackfruit tree, Thura, Aung's apprentice singer, thumped down his overloaded wicker pack of stage curtains and backdrops and the long bamboo poles for the puppet stage. Other members of the puppet troupe settled their precious loads of puppet trunks and musical instruments on the damp red soil, wiped sweat from their faces, and looked back the way they had come.

Around them, pilgrims flooded up the mountain, for this was the sacred home of the King of Nats—and possibly one of the most dangerous places in the country, given King Bodawpaya of Burma had outlawed nat worship. As if the people could fail to honor the nats, at this, the time of the spring pwe—the festival that would thank the nats for their aid during the past difficult year—and seek their blessing for the twelve months ahead.

It was not unthinkable that King Bodawpaya might send soldiers here to arrest everyone and destroy the festival. Whether the king would sanction the destruction of the nat shrine was anyone's guess.

From Aung's vantage, the road wound back down the side of the jungle-clad mountain and then out into fields yellowed under the sun before it leveled off and then rose again to the small town of Kyaukpadaung, shaded from the sun amongst its many trees. Along the road, more pilgrims streamed toward them. The women were clad in their finest blue and yellow and green longyi—their graceful sarongs—while the men's sarongs, called pasos, were blue plaid and knotted at the waist. The women's faces and arms were plastered with sweetly-scented thannaka paste to protect their skin from the sun.

But a silver shimmer filled the air beyond the heat and smoke from the braziers that grilled fish at small kiosks along the road. This time of year, at this place, pork was never cooked, for one of the nats had been Muslim in life. Still, the sweet-scented flesh of the fish sent Aung's stomach growling. It had been long since breakfast and the troupe was too low on funds to buy food from kiosks.

Squinting into the sun through the shimmer, it was almost possible to see figures like clear water striding up the hill. The nats? Or a figment of his ancient imagination and his too-tired eyes? At sixty, Aung was considered very old.

"I thought that we would never get here," Thura said, interrupting Aung's consideration. He was eyeing the huge jackfruit tree leaning over the road. It had glossy leaves and fruit of three-foot-long spiny pods that, when broken open, would give up luscious, yellow, waxy fruit. The tree also gave shade, which was a gift after their long journey across the dusty Pagan plain and their hot climb up the mountain.

Though Aung had seen them many times, on this journey the ancient temples of Pagan had seemed to brood and plot as the troupe passed between them. Perhaps long-dead spirits dwelt among the red brick pagodas, for there were many nats emblazoned on the temples.

The puppet troupe had planned to come to Popa last year, as soon as they finished their performance for King Bodawpaya's wedding. They wished to give thanks to the nats for saving them from what seemed like certain destruction at the hands of the king. But King Bodawpaya had had other ideas and ordered more performances as if he toyed with them. It had held them in Amarapura far longer than they planned.

Finally, they were here, and the silver shimmer in the air and the dancers' presence suggested that the nats had arrived as well.

"Where do we sleep tonight?" Thura asked.

Aung drew his gaze away from the shimmer and sighed. "Desires for the future only make living more difficult."

Aung paraphrased Buddha and Thura dropped his gaze, momentarily ashamed, but he was a good lad with the slim build and high cheekbones of the Chin Hills folk from whence he came.

Aung patted Thura's shoulder and once more contemplated his decision to leave the troupe after this performance. After all these years he would once more shave his head, take up the monk's robe, and return to a monastery.

Like most boys in his village at Inle Lake, as a child he had spent time as a young monk, learning to read and write and the basic lessons of Buddha from the strict monastery teachers. Now he would return and devote his last years to study and contemplation to increase his merit from this life. Thura would take over as principal singer for the troupe. He might be young, but he knew the songs and his voice was strong. Aung just needed to inform the rest of the troupe, who rested beside their packs at the side of the road.

"I think we will set up down by the entrance to the shrines," said Saya Lin, the wiry head puppeteer. Today his usually white shirt was stained pink with sweat and dust. He had pulled up his plaid paso between his knees to form loose, baggy trousers that allowed air around his spindly ankles. His face looked unusually tired, but then the weight of all the mundane tasks of the troupe's welfare had fallen on his broad shoulders since the events in Amarapura.

"Then that is where we will go," Aung said. But it might not be the best place. There were too many of the nat dancers around, inciting the pilgrims. Already young girls were swaying to their raucous music.

But Saya Lin had been with the troupe almost as long as Aung and was now their leader. As boys they had apprenticed together, one to become the most revered puppet master in Burma, the other to become the peerless master of song. It was the wonder of the troupe's magical puppets and the cleverness of their songs that had made them famous throughout King Bodawpaya's lands—and beyond.

Aung went to Saya Lin. "Is there anything that I can do to assume some of your burden, old friend?" He touched Saya Lin's shoulder where he squatted to rest his legs. "It has been a long climb and you carry the Thagyar Min when you are almost as old as I am."

Saya Lin shook his head, but would not look at Aung. "Perhaps explain again why we are here—so that I can see the logic of it this time." He waved his hand at their surroundings. At the nat dancers. "Why bring us from danger into danger, Aung? Wasn't our last close call with death enough for you?"

Saya Lin shook himself and then shouldered his wicker basket and stood. The rest of the troupe followed suit.

"I can still carry a puppet and lead us," he said. He and the puppeteers and musicians trudged, heads bowed with weariness, down the slight incline into to the bowl of land at the foot of mighty Min Mahagiri's shrine.

Aung watched them go. He hated this schism lying between him and his old friend, but it could not be helped. He had pledged to the spirits that the troupe would come. It was not his fault that the king's delay had brought them here at the most risky time of all.

Once, the king of nats, Min Mahagiri, had been a man. He had been incredibly strong and the king of that time had feared that Mahagiri would usurp his throne. So the king had married Mahagiri's sister and used her to lure Mahagiri out of hiding. The king had burned Mahagiri at the stake and his sister had died with him. Both were now spirits of the mountain and, though his worship was outlawed by Burma's current king, he was still revered in household shrines across the country.

His home was here, perched at the top of a thick stone pillar that grew out of the flank of mighty Mount Popa. The pillar towered over the jungle and the landscape beyond. Around its sides, a serpent of 777 covered stairs wound from the base of the pinnacle to the top that was broad enough to hold a number of temples and shrines with gold roofs that glittered in the sunlight. At its base, the jungle gave way to a grassy sward and orchards of papaya, mango, and jackfruit trees. The sweet scent of their fruit filled the air. It was a magnificent place, but their arrival did not relieve Aung's uneasiness.

Perhaps it was the schism with Saya Lin. Or perhaps they were too late making pilgrimage to the nats. Perhaps the nats were angry. Had not Min Mahagiri and his sister slaughtered people in revenge for their own unjust killing? Were others among the nats plotting revenge?

He pressed his palms together, bowed his head, and sent a brief prayer to the nats to apologize for their tardiness.

"Master?"

Aung cut his prayers short.

"Is there a problem? Do you need help?" Thura asked.

"I may be old, but I can walk on these two legs," Aung said and hobbled after his friends, feeling every one of his sixty years. Stepping out of the shadows and into the sun didn't relieve the sense that something large and dark was looking at him.

Whatever it was, it was not his friend.

Chapter 2

At the base of Min Mahagiri's pinnacle, to the left of the white plaster elephants guarding the shrine, and next to a gray-haired fortuneteller who had spread his paraphernalia on a cloth spread on the ground, Saya Lin chose a spot that would allow them to set up their stage with its back to the mountain, far enough from the cadre of nat dancers and their musicians. Behind the stage constructed of bamboo poles, they hung curtains. Inside the curtained enclosure at the rear of the stage, the wicker trunks were stacked and one-by-one they were opened. Inside, the small carved-wood bodies of the puppets gleamed in their finery. Then air shimmered above each one and a puff of fragrant incense filled the air. The white horse, no longer wooden, whinnied and tossed his head. The naga hissed and rattled his scales, his long tongue flicking out of his body, his hood rising about his fanged head. The royal ministers stretched and stood, then huddled together discussing what they saw. The brave prince, Mintha, rose and held out his hand to lovely Minthamee, the princess, as she delicately stepped to the rim of her box. The handmaid suckled her baby.

These were the *yoke thei*—the small dolls carved of the wood of a single Yamani tree. Though they were carved of wood, when they were spirit-inhabited, their wood was coupled with flesh and blood. Each was greeted by their puppeteer, who straightened the puppets' jewel-embossed clothing and brushed out their hair. From the corner, a giggle preceded a commotion as the page puppet, Yamin, barely sixteen inches tall, leapt from his trunk and stuck out his tongue at Zeya, his apprentice puppeteer. Then he scampered across the floor to Aung.

"So." Yamin put his hands on his hips, his blue pantaloons coming only to his knees, his jewel-encrusted vest open on his chest, his twin ponytails bobbing from the crown of his head. "Have you found us a mystery to solve, singer?"

Zeya sent an apologetic look in Aung's direction.

Aung bent at the waist to greet his small friend. "Well met, little master. Well met, indeed, but there is no mystery except the time of our performance, and Saya Lin will soon solve that question."

Yamin sighed and shook his head. "But I thought we agreed that we were going to solve mysteries together. I, for one, thought we were rather good at it. Or I was, at least. You were far too busy trying to avoid me." He tsked.

"And you know that is not the case at all. We worked well together." Not that it hadn't brought problems, too. Yamin was an unruly little spirit who took matters into his hands far more than he should. The troupe had disastrously lost two of its puppets in Amarapura. It was a wonder the yoke thei agreed to perform at all, given they no longer embodied the whole spirit of the Yamani tree from which they'd been made, but somehow with the troupe of puppeteers, Aung and Yamin working together, they had convinced Yamin's brethren to continue to perform.

"Then I suppose that *I* shall just have to find a mystery for us, singer."

"You will do no such thing! To the people you are only carven puppets. They know not of the spirit inhabiting you. You step outside of those curtains and you will bring disaster on all of us. Do you understand?"

Yamin tapped his small bare toes and grinned. "I suppose you know best. This time."

But by the gleam in his eyes, he meant no such thing. The little page would bear close watching.

§

Yamin allowed himself to be cajoled back to his wicker trunk and to have Zeya, who was a reasonable human—young enough to train, at least—check the stitches that held the jewels to his vest. It would not be good to have them fall off in the middle of a performance. But it was Aung that Yamin needed to keep an eye on. The singer was old—like most humans, he'd allowed age to overtake him. This was a problem because old Master Aung didn't moan and tear at his hair when something went wrong. He did something about it.

He *investigated*. It was such an interesting word, an adventure, sometimes with *spies*! Yamin would make sure that he was part of any such investigation, for it had made the long years of his creation so much more interesting, so much better than preening about like Minthamee and that blowhard, Mintha.

When Zeya finished his ministrations, Yamin plopped down on the side of his trunk, kicking the wicker with his small bare heels. Tangles of coiling blue smoke carried the tang of fish cooking on braziers. Offering incense sweetened the air. From beyond the troupe's curtain came the sound of human voices and the cacophonic music and wails of nat wives. Well, that might prove interesting. The wives' performances tore away all the careful decorum of human behavior. From what he'd seen in the past, that was not boring.

Of course the humans always complained afterward, but he didn't have to listen to them. It would be so much *fun* to see what was happening beyond the stupid curtain. The blue sky above the curtained enclosure seemed to be all he was ever allowed.

Well, he for one wasn't about to stay cooped up here.

He looked up at the thick pillar of stone towering directly above their enclosure. At least this time there was more than sky and clouds to see. The mottled pillar rose skyward, as high as the clouds, it seemed. Twisted brown trees scrabbled a hold in the cracks in the stone. A precarious, covered stairway wound around the pinnacle's flanks up to something glittering that he could not quite see. A shimmer around the summit told him all that he needed to know. There were nats there—powerful ones—who were not always predisposed toward their lesser cousins. A single yoke thei, or a yoke thei of an incomplete tree, would be beneath their notice.

Which was probably a good thing given his propensity for trouble—or so Zeya, the other puppets, and the old singer had told him.

The pillar was so tall that it would have a most stupendous view. Even from lower down, one would at least be able to see what was going on with the nat wives and how the silly humans made fools of themselves. It would be grand entertainment, at least for a while, and really held the only very slightest danger of being seen if he stayed among the trees.

He slid off the trunk to the damp red earth, put his hands behind his back, and pretended to practice his dance performance. Of course he didn't need to—a couple of centuries gave plenty of time to perfect it. He concentrated on being small instead and casually edged his way around the curtained compound.

It was not that difficult. The puppeteers were busy making the final checks of the bamboo stage's slope by rolling a coconut across it to see that it only rolled three times. The musicians were out front setting up the dragon drum, the drum and gong circles, and practicing the high-pitched hne. The old singer and the young one were huddled together, probably plotting the most clever songs.

Yamin sidled past them until he reached the curtain by the base of the pinnacle. He ducked under and held his breath, waiting for someone to command him to return.

No one did. He was far too clever at being small and unremarkable.

Steep-sided rock rose above him, tangled in dried weeds and the spindly trunks of the trees. Perhaps it posed a difficult path for a man, but he rubbed his hands together and began to climb. Small fingers and toes were really most excellent for finding one's way up rough stone. He was quickly up amongst the trees above the puppet enclosure and climbed out on a tree branch to survey the area.

Beyond the puppet troupe's curtains, this Popa was the most marvelous place. Brightly-colored blue- and green- and yellow-clad people moved in kaleidoscopic eddies and streams across the green grass. Here and there, cloths had been laid out for families to picnic while enjoying a storyteller's stories. Elsewhere, under colorful awnings, musicians played wild, wailing music. Later, nat wives would sing in their high falsetto, calling out to the nats and the people to join them as they began to dance. At another spot, the nat wife already had the people whirling about in a most ridiculous drunken fashion. Women's longyi rode up their legs. Men's turbans fell off. Long hair whirled about their heads as the gleam of nats enveloped them.

Yamin laughed and clapped his hands at their staggering dance.

An angry chittering came from the pinnacle above him. Yamin stopped laughing. Slowly, he looked up—right into the too-red mouth of a monkey. It had dusky brown-gold fur and very big teeth. It stank of musk. Then the animal leapt for him.

Yamin threw himself from the branch.

The monkey's teeth clacked shut behind him with a power that could surely split wood. Yamin glanced back as the monkey swung after him.

Yamin plunged down the pinnacle, but a hiss and growl came from below. Somehow the beast had gotten between him and the curtained enclosure. Yamin scrambled across the stone face seeking shelter. Looked behind and there was not one monkey, but two, three, five of the creatures, swinging through the trees, leaping across the rocks after him. The vertical stone offered barely toe and finger holds, but the monkeys had no problem.

The grass. If he could get into the grass that grew at the pinnacle's base, perhaps he could hide. At the very worst, perhaps he could take cover amongst the humans. They always had dark nooks and crannies and no great love of monkey raiders.

Below and to one side there was a bright yellow awning and a ring of musical instruments; another nat wife must be going to perform there. There might be some place he could hide, and at the moment no one seemed to be there.

A monkey screamed and leapt from above. Yamin ducked and threw himself down the rocks, tumbling through branches, coming to rest at the base of the yellow awning. The monkeys chittered above him. Beyond, the pwe was full of people—a girl in blue buying lake prawn, a man engaged in conversation with a woman, two men drinking a bottle and laughing. Other people streamed around them.

If anyone looked his way, he'd be seen. A quick check up the hill at the monkeys—still coming—and he ducked inside the golden awning and found himself behind a nat shrine. The golden figure of Mahagiri wore red robes and held a fan and forge hammer. Beneath his feet was a statue of a white elephant, and bouquets of flowers filled the space like gardens. A thin trail of blue smoke rose from incense burning in a small pottery holder.

Yamin slid deeper behind the nat shrine between the awning and the elephant. Beyond the curtain, the monkeys screeched and poked their grasping fingers under the cloth. Yamin stomped on one hand that got too close and heard a most satisfying crunch. The animal screeched, but the hand disappeared. Then a voice yelled and someone chased away the monkeys.

Yamin waited, listening for the monkeys to return or for a human to enter the golden awning. Gradually his breathing slowed and his fear subsided. That had been almost fun. He wasn't sure whether he would do it again, but he might. He dusted off his blue pantaloons. It was strange that the awning was so silent. He inspected the effigy—this Min Mahagiri had a particularly pudgy rear—something that the true Min Mahagiri wouldn't like given the great nat's vanity. The elephant was pitiably small—and he'd always heard that elephants were incredibly tall. Disappointing, really.

He stepped out from behind the effigy and looked out into the covered area under the awning. The yellow cloth turned the grass golden. The musical instruments were a clutter on the ground, the three-foot-tall bamboo slats around the gong circle masking what lay behind the instruments under the awning.

Yamin froze. Stretched out on the ground as if he were sleeping on his back lay the nat wife. The satiny woman's shirt with its flouncy ruffled bottom gave it away. So did the rouge on the pale face above the neck that so clearly had an Adam's apple. Eyes, black as tree shadows, looked up at the awning and Yamin cringed back, praying not to be seen.

Still, the nat wife didn't move. Yamin stepped closer and realized his feet were sinking into wet grass. Blood pooled around the base of the nat effigy and around Yamin's feet.

The man was dead, and for a moment Yamin felt the horror of his situation. Then he brightened.

He had found the old singer another mystery!

Chapter 3

With the afternoon advancing, Aung allowed Thura and Zeya, the puppeteer apprentice, to go explore the festival pwe, with clear instructions not to go near the nat dancers. The last thing the puppet troupe needed was for their apprentices to be possessed by nats.

Aung sipped tea as two of the musicians readied an afternoon meal and the others rested before their evening performance. He considered napping. It would feel good to lie down in the cool mountain air and contemplate a simpler life where he was not charged with composing songs that critiqued the nobles, thereby risking his life and the lives of his troupe mates. It would be—pleasant—to only have to live his life and not concern himself with his betters.

He eyed the bamboo matting. He knew the song of thanks that he had composed for the nats. He knew all the traditional songs by heart and the others would surely not resent his slumber.

The discussions of the puppeteers were a background murmur. The sounds of the pwe swirled beyond the enclosure's curtain, but then the back curtain rustled and a head with two bobbing ponytails appeared, followed by Yamin's body. The little puppet sighed heavily and dusted off his pantaloons.

"I thought I would never make it back, but I found us a mystery!" The troublesome little page hurried up to Aung, almost vibrating with excitement.

"And where have you been? I thought we discussed that you should not be out where you can be seen," Aung said. Adventures could not be allowed. It Yamin was stolen or hurt, then the troupe truly would have to disband because Yamin was crucial in their performances.

Yamin frowned, "If you must know, I have been avoiding monkeys while I sneaked back home. Now are you going to lecture me when we should be solving the mystery? There is a dead body—a nat wife—inside the enclosure with the yellow awning. Someone has killed him."

The little one stood with his hands on his hips. "Well? What do we do, singer?"

Aung shook his head. Given the illicitness of the pwe, they dared not call in the authorities if there truly was a body. But such a matter could not be left, just as one could not leave a body lying about. "Are you certain it was a body and not someone sleeping?"

Yamin rolled his eyes and danced an impatient jig. "I can tell the living from the dead, singer. He lay in a pool of crimson. I, for one, do not believe humans normally sleep in blood."

Aung nodded slowly. "I agree with you. That does not sound good."

Yamin uncrossed his arms and caught the hem of Aung's paso in his hands. "I can take you there—if you can climb under the curtain." The excitement was back again.

Aung shook his head and loosed his paso fabric from Yamin's grip. "I don't need to slip away from the troupe. Now you stay here like a good page and I will go have a look."

He looked pointedly at Yamin until finally the small one nodded.

"I only wanted to see, so I climbed the mountain—until monkeys came after me. I only took shelter under the awning." Yamin gazed up at him with soulful eyes.

"You scamp. Don't play innocent with me. You never should have been out there in the first place. Now go and pluck the grass from your hair and dust off your clothes or poor Zeya will receive Saya Lin's wrath."

Aung hobbled out of the enclosure and looked left and right. The number of people arriving for the pwe had tripled. He'd known the festival was popular, but this was as if all the leaves in a forest had fallen in one pile. People jostled against one another. They flooded around the performance areas. They feasted on food from the kiosk braziers. If a man had been murdered, it would be difficult to find the killer; but surely someone must have seen something. Finding out what would be the difficulty.

A grey-bearded fortuneteller and his apprentice were reading fortunes on a plaid paso they had spread on the ground next to the puppet stage. Beyond them, a yellow awning showed above a tumble of stone that had long ago fallen from Min Mahagiri's pinnacle. Aung nodded at the puppeteers, who were busy hanging curtains and putting the final touches on the stage, and stepped into the crowd, shoving in the direction he wanted to go.

He allowed the current of the crowd to direct him until it spit him out by the yellow awning—a clear sign that unseen forces wanted him to come here. From the front it looked ordinary enough. A typical nat wife's enclosure with the drums and gong circle ready to release their cacophonous music.

The sweetness of incense joined the mélange of cooking meat, ripe fruit, and sun-heated bodies. Beyond the yellow awning, a larger awning of blue and white stripes made a bold statement. Similar musical instruments suggested another nat wife.

For all they were endangered by the king's edicts, apparently they were prepared to take the chance to perform at the pwe. Oddly, though most of the nat wives and musicians were busy readying themselves for the pwe, there was no sign of anyone associated with the golden awning.

"Hello?" he called into the yellow enclosure. No one answered.

"Hello?" A little louder.

"He's not there," a voice said and then a face with rough cheeks poked through the neighboring blue-and-white curtain. "I think they all went out a while ago."

"Thank you, friend." Aung inclined his head, but when the nat wife withdrew, he stepped past the drums and the bamboo ring of the gong circle.

It was as Yamin had described: on the patch of earth before the gold-faced nat effigy lay the body of the nat dancer, his arms outstretched. Coal black hair spread about his shoulders. His dark eyes peered up at the sky with a startled look at his unexpected demise. Aung bowed his head and sent a brief prayer to speed the man's spirit on its way to its next incarnation and to the nat to forgive his intrusion.

His knees popped as he crouched down beside the man. Yamin was right. The man was undoubtedly dead. But there was something else, as well. He recognized the man.

Knees cracking, he stood and shuffled out from under the awning. Nai Zaya, one of the more discreet of the puppeteers, was fussing with the puppet stage background. Aung caught his eye, waved him over.

"There is a problem," Aung said softly. "The nat dancer of this awning lies dead inside. Get word to Saya Lin and tell him the organizer of the pwe must be called so the body can be dealt with."

Nai Zaya's eyes grew round, but he bowed to Aung and hurried away.

Hopefully the body could be dealt with, with the least fuss necessary. There would be concern over a death at the festival. He went back to the body and considered the blood-spattered marigolds that hung from the blood-soaked elephant pedestal. Not just a death, a murder—and a violent one.

A Death in Passing

As Yamin had said, they had a mystery.

§

Yamin sat on the side of his wicker basket, kicking it with his heels. The old man had left him to investigate the dead body without even trying to take Yamin with him. It was most distressing—almost as if the old singer did not wish to continue their investigative partnership.

In the fading afternoon light inside the curtained compound, the puppeteers fussed over their charges. The yoke thei fretted and haughtily demanded their puppeteers be more gentle. All the jewels on their clothing glittered like the eyes of little birds. Everyone tried to go on with their business as if everything was normal, but everyone knew that something bad had happened. A body had been found. Something mysterious had occurred.

And he was left here to mull over these thoughts like a cow chewing cud, while the singer got to do everything exciting—and—and investigative! It wasn't fair—at all!

When the curtain stirred, he leapt to his feet and scrambled onto the top of his basket. When the old singer pushed inside, he leapt down and stalked over to the old man to block his progress.

"Well? Do you believe me now? You found my body, didn't you?" He tapped his toes on the red earth.

"Yes," the old singer nodded. "We found a dead nat wife just as you described." He shook his head. "He was so young."

"And I suppose you know who killed him, too. You had all the adventure and left me out of the fun."

The old singer bent down. "Are you pouting, Yamin?"

"No!" he said crossly. He threw his shoulders back and lifted his chin to look the singer eye-to-eye. "I, for one, am most certainly not pouting."

"Good, because there is a mystery to solve and it is time for you and me to consult." The singer hobbled away to a stool on a bamboo mat in the corner and sank down, his old joints cracking like dry wood.

Yamin hurried after him.

"So? What did you learn? What did you see?"

But the old man only waved his question away. "Sit, Yamin. Please. I think it may be more helpful for you to tell me what you saw when you discovered the body. That is most likely where the evidence of his killer would be found. Tell me again what you saw. Who was around?"

Yamin straightened and checked over his shoulders. Were the other yoke thei looking? Did they notice the esteem with which the old singer held him? It was hard being the puppet carved in the likeness of a child so that no one took him seriously, even though he was of an age with all the other puppets. Were they not tree mates?

But *some* yoke thei were flighty, insular folk. Aside from their puppeteers, they paid little attention to the goings on of humans. At the moment, they were too busy being cosseted by their puppeteers as the head of the puppeteers ordered everyone around. Yamin sighed and turned back to the singer.

"I told you. I was on the pinnacle looking down over the pwe—it was very interesting with all the people and the spirits intertwined, I must say. There were people going every which way. Then the monkeys chased me, and I fell and hid inside the yellow awning. At first I didn't think anyone was there."

"Did you see anyone outside the awning? Anyone nearby? Anyone leaving in a hurry? Did you see the nat wife's musicians?" The old man's face was intense—and worried.

"What's the matter, singer? You look like you have just swallowed something sour—or poison."

"This is no game, Yamin." The old man lowered his voice. "A man has died. One who was beloved of the spirits. There is no telling what may happen now. The great nats may rain ill-luck on everyone here until the culprit is found."

"But... even us? We are yoke thei—are nats ourselves. They would not harm the puppet troupe."

The old man shook his head and sighed. When he spoke again, it was in a whisper. "I pray you are right, my friend. These are very risky times."

§

The apprentices, Thura and Zeya, were missing.

Time ticked and the day passed to evening as the troupe prepared for their performance. The afternoon had been marred with men removing the body to a mountainside monastery just below the pwe grounds and with the mutterings of the villagers attending the festival. There were rumors that the man had been cut down because he had affronted Min Mahagiri, and people questioned whether they should stay at the pwe. Most of all there were mutterings that the culprits had been seen escaping down the mountain and that they must be caught to pay for their deed.

Above their curtained area the sky had gone gray, though the westering sun clawed long fingers of light across the sky. Beyond the curtained enclosure, the competing music of the living nat wives rose in a cacophonous noise that set Aung's head aching. Inside the enclosure, the usual pre-puppet show bedlam kept even Yamin occupied. But worry had placed a sharp edge on everyone's temper.

"I don't understand what has happened to them," Aung said to Saya Lin for at least the tenth time. "Neither Nai Thiha nor U Myint saw any sign of them when they went looking."

Saya Lin pulled Aung aside to the back corner of the enclosure. "And I will say, again, that you should not have given them permission to go." The master puppeteer's face was rigid. "Just what are we to do? We have a performance and the young fools have not returned. They have probably gotten drunk on toddy wine and are sleeping it off somewhere. Tomorrow, when they come creeping back, they will have to deal with me!"

Aung hung his head. "I am sorry, old friend. I had thought Zeya had your permission and so granted Thura mine. The young scamps fooled me." Yet another reason he should retire if he could not see through two apprentices' subterfuge.

Saya Lin closed his eyes. "Is it not bad enough that you forced us to come here to make obeisance to the nats against the king's edicts? Is it not ill enough that it is during this pwe when not only the nat wives are here, but everyone goes mad while they attend? No, you dragged us into this! Another dead body practically at the edge of our stage!"

Saya Lin scanned the flurry of puppeteers and musicians, the small glittering yoke thei in their midst. "This troupe is not your plaything, Aung. We are not here to simply do your bidding, no matter that you saved us in Amarapura."

Aung nodded his head in tired agreement. It was all true, though it hurt to have his old friend lecture him. "I recognized the dead man. Did you?"

"How would I know him?"

Aung lowered his voice. "I do not know his name, but I believe we've met him. It was when we were last in Arakan. The last village pwe had brought in a nat dancer of some renown. He was quite young, but beloved of Taungbyon the elder, if I remember rightly. He called down the nats and set most of the village dancing. I had not seen the like if it before, though old tales tell of entire cities dancing from the spirits' joy. A most impressive man."

Saya Lin either did not remember or did not want to. He looked back to the puppeteers and puppets. "Given everything that has happened, by rights I should simply order the stage taken down and our immediate withdrawal from this place."

The strain showed around Saya Lin's eyes.

"But you will not because you understand that propitiating the nats is the right thing to do after they saved us. They hold too much power over men's fate."

"So does the king," Saya Lin hissed. "Or have you forgotten the loss of our friend?" Their disastrous trip to Amarapura had resulted in more than the murder of the puppet who was the effigy of the human king. It had taken its toll of the humans as well.

Saya Lin shook himself and turned back to the show preparations. "We will perform, U Myint will dance Yamin tonight, and you must sing Thura's parts. But let it be said that any ill that befalls this troupe will be on your head. Tomorrow we will leave if the gods—and your nats—are willing." He stomped away into the bustle of puppeteers and greeted the Thagyar Min—the celestial king—with a bow.

Feeling the sting of Saya Lin's anger, Aung went outside the curtain to climb up into the wings of the stage. A soft pillow had been set to ease Aung's old bones and he eased himself down, cross-legged. His knees and hips ached and it was becoming increasingly hard to complete his duties. He would just get through this performance and then he could rest. That was the thought that kept him going. Just propitiate the nats and then go home to the monastery.

But the fact that the dead man had been a nat dancer of some renown was not auspicious. Not auspicious at all. In fact, it sent a sense of doom throbbing through Aung's breast deeper that the dragon drum's beat.

And then there was Thura. Like a gaping wound, the space Thura usually occupied across the puppet stage from him yawned empty. Saya Lin's concern that the young men were drunk somewhere was the least of their worries. There was a murderer about. What if the boys had seen something and been killed?

He clamped down on that worry and looked beyond the stage. The troupe's musicians were settled with their instruments at the base of the stage, the huge dragon drum almost as tall as the stage, with the drum suspended from the belly of a brightly painted, gilt-wood dragon carved so cleverly that its coils appeared to move. Beyond the musicians, instead of blankets spread with mothers and children awaiting the performance, men and women staggered past, drunk on toddy wine and the nats' influence.

Aung shivered. Perhaps Saya Lin had been right. What good could coming here do them? They would not be paid for the performance like they would at a normal pwe. It was only if you believed in the nats that it made sense to come here to gain the nats' favor, their blessings, and to thank them for saving the troupe from total destruction. It had been such a near thing. The king could have ordered their deaths at any time, but the nats had seemingly interceded. Still, Saya Lin's faith in the nats seemed to have waned.

As if Aung's thought had brought forth the man, Saya Lin popped his head through the curtain at Aung's shoulder. "I'm sorry. I should not have said what I did. I know you only think of our welfare."

Aung nodded. "I am sorry, too, old friend. I know the great strain you've been under. I will try to support you better." He smiled and Saya Lin clasped his arm as old friends will.

"Sing well. We'll show those drunkard apprentices what a true performance is. I may question whether we need Thura at all as long as you can sing."

Aung nodded again and Saya Lin pulled back behind the curtain, but worry gelled in Aung's belly. If Thura did not return, there was no possible way he could retire. He could not leave the troupe without a singer, for a puppet troupe without songs was no troupe at all.

Out in the gathering darkness, the nat wives were busy. By firelight and torchlight they danced with arms outstretched in court dancer poses, their feet shuffling in the mincing steps, their voices rising in wailing songs that called the spirits down to inhabit them and the bodies of their drunken audience. Here a young woman hiked up her longyi and whirled in place, her hair coming loose from its careful coil at the back of her head. There a man let his turban fall and his long hair swung around him as he swooped and danced in a caricature of a bird.

As if these people would even notice the more subtle magic of the yoke thei.

Then the puppet troupe's drummer struck the dragon drum and the huge hollow boom reverberated through Aung's belly. The hne and the gong circle took up their song and joined the morass of music around the pwe. On stage, the lovely votaress in her golden longyi danced onto the stage. She carried with her a bowl of miniature coconut, banana, and rice in effigy of the real offering set at the corner of the stage. The votaress wove and danced as a real woman would—a product not of the puppet strings that everyone could see, but of the magical, gossamer strings that hung amongst her raven hair. For the yoke thei were an unruly lot, as any nat spirit was known to be, but the gossamer strings in the hands of a skilled puppeteer allowed the puppet and the puppeteer to become as one, thus the perfect performances were possible.

Aung sang the traditional song of offering, but his voice cracked at one point. Usually Thura picked up the song when the little alchemist came on stage and performed his wonders, but this time Aung continued to sing. His throat ached. The alchemist tossed his wand into the air and caught it again. He leapt and danced and whirled and then was gone, leaving an empty stage and a much needed pause in the song until the hne took up a playful tune, and Yamin danced onto the stage.

The page was a jolly sort who usually sang in Thura's lilting voice. Tonight Aung's ragged falsetto sang of the apparent prowess of an old king's loins, for the latest word before the troupe had left Amarapura was that the newest bride of the king was pregnant. A happy day. Or it should be. But the way that Aung had composed the song, the troupe's few listeners began to laugh. A few passersby stopped to listen and then more and more.

Perhaps they would get an audience yet.

When Yamin was done, Mintha and Minthamee danced on stage, enchanting the crowd with their beauty and young love. Aung sang both parts—straining his voice around the lover's song of yearning that had the poignant power to cut through the throaty songs of the spirit wives. Yes, the performance would unfold in honor of the nats and tomorrow, as Saya Lin said, once the apprentices returned they would take their leave. He relaxed into the performance.

The scream jarred him out of it, the song's words failing to reach his lips so the musical beat went on without him.

A man's shout, joined by others, cut through all the performances so the madhouse of music jangled to a stop—even the hne that gave music to Minthamee's grace. The prince and princess puppets staggered to a stop on stage and looked around them, confused. The musicians turned in their seats as a gray-haired woman pushed her way through the crowd, her torch-lit face a mass of anger.

"They caught them! The caught the killers! They bring them back for justice!"

Chapter 4

Beyond the puppet enclosure, the tide of human voices swelled. Far away at the other end of the pwe, the last wail and honk of a nat dancer's musicians stuttered to silence.

From his waiting place on a shelf behind the stage, Yamin eased sideways and parted the curtain to peer into the darkness beyond the puppet enclosure. Torchlight flickered and painted the human faces a red more gaudy than any puppet rouge. Beyond them the mountain lifted in a massive darkness that swallowed the stars. Following down the road from the mountainside into the pwe came a mass of dimly lit figures.

"That cannot be good." The old singer's voice drifted through the curtain from the wing of the stage. The curtains billowed as the old singer climbed down from his perch.

The puppeteers and musicians stopped what they were doing and Yamin eased down from the shelf where the yoke thei were supposed to wait, and slid to the curtain edge by the old man's side.

Loud voices stirred like currents in the night air. Torchlight flickered and flared. Above them, the pinnacle seemed to inhale and exhale a silvery glow.

"Something's happening," he whispered and edged through the curtain. He caught the hem of the old singer's faded blue paso in his hand.

The voices coalesced in the darkness, yelling something unintelligible, which was to be expected given these were humans and not even puppeteers. Then a single voice rose above the rest.

"Killers! You brought killers into our midst! You must pay for the death!" it bellowed. Then the other voices joined to become a chorus singing out that single demand: "Killers must pay! Killers must pay!"

"What are they talking about?" the thin master puppeteer said to the singer.

"I've no idea," the singer said. He reached down and gently eased his paso out of Yamin's fingers. "Stay inside the curtain. This could be dangerous and I've told you before that you cannot be seen."

Yamin went to object, for he wasn't afraid of danger—not at all, though he couldn't quite recall anything dangerous that he'd ever done. But the old singer gave him a stern look that might even promise some sort of reprimand if Yamin didn't do as bid. Well, he'd obey for the moment—at least until he could see whether it was to his advantage. He nodded and ducked inside the curtain as the two humans stepped away from the stage.

Yamin plopped down on the bamboo mat, fighting back his frustration. Sometimes there really were disadvantages to being a magical creature.

But he wasn't going to think about that.

§

Aung and Saya Lin stepped past the musicians' circle out into the night-bound clearing. The torchlight stained the angry faces of the crowd that had come to a stop in front of them. One man faced them, a burly fellow with a plain gray turban. He wore a simple plaid paso, but the fabric was new and a leather cord held a small golden Buddha image around his neck. A rich man, then. Perhaps the organizer of the pwe or one of the restaurant owners who could hold some sway with the crowd.

"What is it you want?" Saya Lin asked. His voice carried over the crowd as he drew himself up. "You disturb the yoke thei performance."

The wealthy man glanced over his shoulder as if checking the solidarity of his followers. Apparently he was satisfied with what he saw, for when he turned back to Saya Lin, his face was grim. "You have a death to answer for. You brought the killers to this pwe!"

Saya Lin turned a shocked look in Aung's direction.

Bewildered, Aung shook his head in response. Saya Lin turned back to the man.

"The members of our troupe were busy preparing for our performance. They cannot have killed anyone."

The man shook his head. "Then you disown these youngsters?"

The crowd parted and two battered figures were shoved forward to their knees.

Aung's breath caught in his throat. Saya Lin swore.

Sixteen-year-old Thura looked up at him through a tangle of hair, terror in his gaze. Only a year older, silver tears ran down moon-faced Zeya's cheeks. A bloody wound oozed on his forehead. The two youngsters huddled together.

"This afternoon I gave you permission to explore the pwe," Aung whispered.

Saya Lin's face paled. "It could not be them. They are good lads—mostly."

"But they were out there," the crowd's leader said.

"I saw them running from the golden awning," said a man shoving forward to stand behind the boys.

"Neither youth would do such a thing," Saya Lin said, raising his voice to the crowd.

The mass of people sputtered and growled.

The wealthy man stepped forward. "Can you not see that this crowd is on the brink of chaos—too much liquor, too much pent up inside them, and now this. They planned to tear your stage apart, but I talked them down. I said you may have not known the evil you brought with you."

"But neither lad is a killer. This cannot be true," Saya Lin said.

"Then you will need to explain the blood on their clothing and on their hands." The wealthy man's face was unrelenting. "You say these boys are innocent. All I can do is try to keep them safe until morning, when the drink wears off and saner heads can prevail."

Saya Lin shook his head. "We will keep them secure here."

"And risk the rabble? I doubt any of you will see tomorrow." He went to turn away.

"Wait!" Aung stopped him and turned to Saya Lin. "Perhaps—perhaps they should go with him, and I will go as well, to ensure their safety. Look at the crowd's faces, old friend. The night and toddy wine have washed sanity free of them."

It was true. Too many of the men were wild-eyed and sweating. The women were wanton with their clothes tugged loose and their hair tangled about their shoulders. All of them had gazes glazed by torchlight and wine and some held the spirits' glow on their skin—still half possessed. This was not a crowd you could reason with.

Saya Lin's strained expression said he read the same thing.

He inhaled and sighed and then said in an overloud voice. "I will leave our two apprentices in your safekeeping for the night. The master singer will go with them to ensure they receive no more of your gentle treatment. I hold all those here accountable for their wellbeing, for they are performers in the king's own royal puppet troupe. We will sort this out in the morning."

Saya Lin glowered at Aung, clearly not happy at events and that they would not be leaving as he'd planned.

"Tell the crowd to disperse and then you can lead us where you will," Aung said. With a nod he returned through the curtain.

"You can't leave the boys with that crowd!" said U Myint, who had once been the Garuda's puppeteer. "They're as likely to string them up as keep them safe." The poor man clearly still reeled from the loss of his small charge.

"And so I'm going with them," Aung said. A tug on his paso forced him to look down. Yamin stood with his arms akimbo, glaring up at him. "And what about our discussion? How are we to solve the mystery if we can't investigate?"

"Yamin, this is not the time." He tugged his paso fabric free, but Yamin grabbed it again.

"So say you, but you walk into danger without me to help you."

"Yamin, you are a puppet. Here is where you are meant to be, not out solving murders," U Myint said with a glance at Aung that said the singer was at fault for encouraging the little yoke thei. "Stay here and let no one see you. You watch, Master Saya Lin and Master Aung will have your apprentice back by morning."

It was a confident enough speech, but Aung wasn't sure it was worth the breath used on it. He bent down to Yamin. "Truly, little one. Our investigation is not over. I need you to think hard about everything you saw today. It is more crucial now than ever before—in fact, the lives of our friends may depend upon it."

Yamin's gaze narrowed as if he didn't quite believe, but then he nodded. "All right. I, for one, have an important task. See you complete yours as well, singer, for I have grown fond of my apprentice puppeteer. He has a sense of humor."

Back outside, Thura and Zeya now huddled together on their feet. It was a comfort to see that at least some of the crowd had dispersed, but too many angry faces were still aimed in their direction.

"You wait; I will come for you both tomorrow morning and we will sort this foolishness out," Saya Lin said with a pat on the shoulder for both young men. "See you take care, old friend," he said quietly to Aung. "I fear this will be dangerous."

Aung only nodded and set out with the two youngsters, following behind the wealthy man. The night reeked of sour sweat and anger as the crowd opened up to let them pass. When Aung glanced behind, there was no way back through the darkness.

Chapter 5

The curtain settled behind the old singer and Yamin's hands ground to fists. It wasn't fair at all that the old man had all the adventures and he, for one, was going to do something about it. Besides, something bad was happening. Clearly someone with some sense needed to deal with that.

Around him the other puppeteers were talking in that worried way they had. The other yoke thei were still complaining about the abrupt ending of their show. *They* didn't seem to understand at all. He would probably be doing the same thing except that he had learned to *pay attention*. That was the only way you solved a mystery, and apparently something his tree mates had forgotten. Was that what happened with age to yoke thei? Would they become so disconnected from the world around them that eventually they would just fade away into irrelevance?

Not him. Certainly not him, for he got to sing the most important songs that commented on things going on in the world.

When it seemed that the puppeteers had forgotten him, Yamin eased carefully to the curtain and ducked out when no one was looking.

The night was cool and the breeze stirred the murky scent of Mount Popa's jungles around him as the puppeteers' voices rose behind him. Across the grassy slope at the base of Min Mahagiri's pillar, the crowd was dispersing, with a few determined souls departing the clearing for some kind of trail leading down into the trees. Here and there, small cook fires flared, but the wild music and the dancing had ended. The murder had ended the wild celebration of the nats. They would not be happy.

He glanced up at the top of the pillar where the silvery glow caught the moonlight around the temples and shrines. Though the air was sweet with incense and flowers, it could not hide an undertone of iron. Yamin shivered. Min Mahagiri was not happy, and though he was often an unhappy nat who needed frequent offerings to keep ill luck at bay, at the moment his discontent verged into anger.

That was not a good thing, for there was no telling what might happen to those around him.

"Have a care, Great One. There are people trying to put things to right. Like me and the singer."

Keeping to the shadows, he set out across the clearing. Muttering men and women lay in uneasy slumber on longyi spread on the soft grass surrounding fires. Shadowy figures moved around the awnings where the nat wives talked softly with their musicians. The silvery glow of nat possession still lay lightly on the nat wives, their voices altered as if two voices spoke as one. Perhaps tomorrow they would return to their singing and the spirits would smile on them.

He snuck past them all, confident that his small size helped him remain unremarked. After all, if no one *expected* him to exist, it was highly unlikely that they would *expect* to see him.

Across the clearing, two man-high, carved stones marked a path that dove deep into the trees on the side of the mountain. The path was dark, for the leaves kept the moonlight out and the jungle breathed with the sound of leaves and the trickle of water. He paused, listening, and heard the distant sound of human voices, but beyond the humans, there was something else there.

"Mighty Taw Saun, kin, I enter your world on your sufferance." He bowed with his hands palm together before his face. The Taw Saun was the spirit of the forest, the guardian of trees and all manner of beasts who lived there. To enter a forest without acknowledging the Taw Sawn was to court ill luck of the worst kind.

He tiptoed down the path and followed it as it wound down among the trees, only to end at the open gate leading into a moonlit courtyard of high stone walls. An ornate, stilted teak building with carved, naga-dragon-shaped eaves stood in the center, and from its windows leaked sweet incense that caught the light and coiled like serpents. From across the courtyard came the sound of soft voices that included the old singer's. A low drone came from the building in the center of the courtyard. From the forest beside him came a soft whimper.

Yamin edged in amid the leaves. Who was there? Had they seen him? The old singer might be too bossy, but he was probably right that Yamin shouldn't be seen.

Silently he eased the leaves apart and spied a girl crumpled amid the bushes. She was clad in a faded longyi with an unusual design of flowers and fish, with a plain blue blouse that showed much wear. Her long dark hair she had pulled around her face so he could not see her features even though his eyesight was far better than the old singer's.

She looked up suddenly as if she was aware of him, and silver tears trailed down her cheeks as if she held nat magic within herself.

Yamin froze.

"Is—is someone there?" She had a soft voice, with an accent he had not heard before, but then, he was not exactly an expert in human speech.

He held still and didn't answer, for there was no telling what an upset human girl would do and he was not about to find out.

Her hopeful gaze blindly sought among the air above her. "Tet? Is it you? Have you come back from the dead already to see me?" Then her hope faded from her face. She shook her head. "I am a fool. He has not yet found his next life."

With a sigh, she picked herself up off the ground, wiped leaves off her longyi, and palmed tears off her face. She turned toward the courtyard gate as if considering, then shook her head and stepped past where Yamin crouched and onto the path. She trudged back toward the pinnacle and clearing.

Most interesting. He waited until she was gone and then stood. Just why she was crying he wasn't sure, but it seemed that someone had died. The nat wife, perhaps?

A clue! He had a clue that no one else had!

He danced a little in place and then faced the courtyard with his hands on his hips.

"So, master singer, just what have you learned this night?"

§

The monastery that lay in Mount Popa's shadow housed twenty-five monks and offered hospitality and a hostel to pilgrims who found their way to Min Mahagiri's abode. Seated on the cold stone floor of one of the pilgrim cells, Aung faced Thura and Zeya. Outside, in the darkness, stood two guards. Setting aside the bowl of clean water he had used to wash Zeya's wounds, Aung leaned forward, keeping his voice low. "So, young fools, what have you done?"

Thura and Zeya looked at each other like conspirators.

"Thura! Don't look at him, look at me. Tell the truth. What happened today that these villagers would believe that you killed the nat wife?"

Thura's shoulders collapsed and he looked at his hands. "I am most sorry, Master. It—it was horrible. Zeya and I—we went out for our adventure around the pwe. I know you said not to, but I hoped to meet a nat wife, to see what they could tell me of my future."

"But all of the wives were busy," Zeya picked up the story, his round face having lost the jolly humor that allowed him to manage the troublesome Yamin so well. "They were singing and dancing and calling to the villagers. People were getting drunk, and I knew that if we took a drink, Saya Lin would skin us alive."

"Then we noticed the yellow awning," Thura said. "It looked like another of the nat wife enclosures, but there were no musicians about and no singing and dancing, so we thought that we might have a chance to talk to the wife." He looked at Zeya, and Thura's thin face was pale, even under his darker Chin complexion. He swallowed. "We couldn't see anyone there. We called out and no one answered, so we thought we'd look around." He glanced down at his hands. "It was stupid, but we were curious, so we stepped inside—and that was when we saw him."

The night breeze hissed through the monastery stone and the monks continued to drone from their prayer room. Thura's pleading gaze came up to Aung.

"You must understand. When I saw him, I went to my knees to try to help him, but he was already dead. My hands and knees got covered in blood and when I was going to call for help, there were so many people who seemed to be looking in our direction. I knew they'd think we'd killed him. So we decided the best thing we could do was to leave. We couldn't come back to the troupe because that would bring you trouble and the troupe—you and Saya Lin—already have so much to deal with. We—we thought that if we went down the mountain, then we could meet with you again when you left the pwe. We would explain then and by then we would have washed our clothes clean of blood."

Zeya hung his head. "I am sorry, Master Aung. We were foolish."

Aung sat back and considered them. Blood still stained Thura's paso and fingernails, though the lad continued to try to scrape them clean. "Fools indeed. To think you could find a dead man, run away, and have no one notice."

"But they've misinterpreted what we did!" Thura protested. "We didn't kill anyone!"

Zeya nodded vehemently beside him.

"Except perhaps yourselves unless we can sort this mess out," Aung said. He closed his eyes and inhaled the incense- and teak-scented air. He wanted tea. He wanted the comfort of his bed, or even better, a cell like this to call his own at the small Inle Lake monastery that he'd begun to dream of.

"Then perhaps I can be of help!"

Aung almost collapsed in surprise as Yamin leapt into the room.

"Ta da!" the infernal page said. Then he bowed politely.

Aung grabbed him and pulled him away from the open door. "Are you truly so bent on the destruction of us all that you would come here? You could have been seen! The guards still could see you!" He turned his body to mask the problematic little puppet from the guardians beyond the door.

"What are you doing here, Yamin?" Zeya asked.

"You shouldn't be here at all," Aung repeated.

"Well, I, for one, at least know who my true friends are," he said brushing off his vest and paso after freeing himself from Aung's grasp. He gave a winning smile to his puppeteer. "I see they haven't killed you yet. That's good. Very good. I'm here to help. So what have you learned?" Yamin asked, turning to the old singer.

Aung rolled his eyes. "That young page yoke thei and apprentices are entirely more trouble than they are worth."

"Well, that's not a particularly helpful attitude, singer. Not when I bring you a clue, which is more than you've done for me." He crossed his arms and tapped his toes. "Now I must decide whether I'll tell you or not."

Aung held up his hand to forestall the little puppet's ramblings. "I was just hearing their story."

Shrugging, Yamin plopped down on his belly and rested his chin in his hands.

Thura and Zeya repeated their story for Yamin. When they were done, the page looked up at Aung.

"Tell me, singer, are all young humans so foolish?"

Aung couldn't help but sigh and shake his head. Young humans, young puppets—at least the young-looking ones—were apparently much the same. "I hope not."

"Most unfortunate," Yamin said frowning. "Strange that people saw them and not the real killer."

Aung sat back and frowned. "A most astute observation, my small friend. If these people saw our apprentices, they should have seen the killer, too."

"Then why didn't they say something?" Thura asked. "Why blame us?"

"Indeed," Aung said, then thought about it. "Strange, too, that there was no sign of the nat wife's musicians. What say you, Yamin? You have good ideas."

The page preened. Then he scratched the base of one of the ponytails on the crown of his head. "Perhaps they did not know what they saw. Or perhaps they did not wish to see it."

"Wish to see it?" said Zeya. "How can you wish not to see something? You either see it or you don't."

Yamin frowned. "These ones need to learn that the first thing is to examine all the options and *then* examine whether they are right or wrong—not discount them while they are still newborn ideas."

Zeya sat back, apparently chastised.

"Why would they not know what they saw?" Thura asked. "And where could the musicians be?"

Aung closed his eyes and thought. "Perhaps the musicians killed him and escaped." He sighed. "Many people are so taken up with their own lives that they don't see what goes on around them. It is common in this life of problems that we become consumed with our own needs. Perhaps the action that they saw was so common that they did not recognize what they were seeing." He arched his brow at the apprentices and they at least had the grace to look embarrassed.

"Why would a person not wish to see something?"

"That's easy," Yamin said. "The sight is unpleasant."

"He's right," Aung said, "as far as it goes. Think: A poor man sees a rich man drop his purse, but he recounts the tale as seeing only the purse on the ground.

Soon be begins to believe his own tale and so the truth has been unseen."

"But he told a lie," Thura said.

"He told something that he now believes. If these folk at the pwe do not want to believe the truth, then the truth may cease to be unless we show it to them." Aung looked up at the sky. The night was failing, a glow to the east proof that the day was transcendent—or would be—and with the dawn came judgment. He stood. "I must find your accusers and those who were near the nat wife's awning and speak to them about what they truly saw. And the musicians. We must learn what became of them."

Yamin scrambled up beside him. "It is always most satisfying to discuss an investigation with you, singer. But I have a clue for you, too. That is why I am here."

By his innocent expression that wasn't quite true, but...

"A clue, Yamin?" Aung leaned down to the page.

Yamin's ponytails bobbed as he nodded. "A very good one, too. On my way here I happened upon a girl crying in the forest. She called for someone named Tet and asked if he'd come back from the dead so soon. Then she called herself a fool and left." He grinned up at Aung. "I think that Tet must be the name of the dead man."

A memory of the long ago pwe in Arakan came flooding back. The nat wife was dancing across the clearing from the yoke thei stage and the village headman was standing beside Aung telling him how proud he was that he had been able to prevail upon the preeminent Arakanese nat wife and dancer—Tet.

He glanced once more at the lightening sky. "Of course you are right. Come, Yamin. We must get you out of here before the sunrises. Here on the mountain there are too few places for even one as small as you to hide."

Just as, apparently, Tet, the nat wife, had found no place to hide. No place to run. And so he was dead.

Chapter 6

Yamin scampered after Aung as the singer distracted the guards. The old singer also told the guards that he held them responsible for the young men's safety. Then he left, even though Yamin thought the guards looked rather shady. He didn't want anything to happen to his young puppeteer. And the young singer brought just the right bit of fun into the words he sang. Yamin liked that about him. Like Zeya, the youngster might even be *trainable*—unlike the old singer.

Yamin kept to the shadows and scurried out the gate as Aung kept the men occupied, then Yamin hid in the forest much as the girl had done while he waited for the old singer to leave.

When the old man hobbled out the gate, Yamin revealed himself. "Here I am. I was just thinking, singer. Why was the girl crying before the gate of the monastery? If she cared for Tet, shouldn't she be with the lot who plot vengeance on our apprentices?"

"An interesting thought. Perhaps she knows something. We'll need to find her, but in the meantime we need to discuss who might want to kill the nat wife."

Yamin danced a little dance. "That is my kind of game. Shall you begin, or shall I?"

He trotted after the old singer as he trudged up the slope of the path toward the clearing.

Aung nodded down at him. "The man was from Arakan. I remember when I saw him before. His songs always called down the nats with power, but he also called on them to free his people from the yoke of the Burmese king. There is no love between the people of Arakan and Burma now. Not since King Bodawpaya stole their golden Mahamuni Buddha and brought it north to Amarapura. Tet's songs would not be popular here in Burma."

Yamin thought about it. "So someone might have killed him for his politics?"

Aung looked down at him. "You surprise me, Yamin. I did not think you knew that word!"

"And now you insult me?" Yamin stopped with his hands on his hips, for he was wiser than anyone ever gave him credit for—hadn't he proved that on their last case? "That was not kindly said, master singer. You take that back."

Aung bowed his head."I apologize. I just had not expected to hear a yoke thei speak of the politics of men. But you are quite right. Politics could be a reason."

For the moment satisfied, Yamin nodded. A night moth fluttered by and he leapt for it, catching the edge of its velvet wing. The velvet came off and discolored his hands, soft as the most tender leaf in spring. "It could be for love, singer. There was that girl."

"And he was reputed to be the greatest nat wife in this generation. That could breed jealousy," Aung said.

Yamin scampered after the moth. "There are always so many reasons to kill a human. It's a surprise there are so many of you left."

The moth darted out into the open clearing and Yamin stopped and waited for the old singer to join him. Dawn filled the clearing with misty light, revealing the spread of mats across the clearing and the slumbering bodies of far too many people for him to safely skirt around. Already mothers were up dealing with their fussing children. Old men sat smoking and chewing betel around a new fire, their orange lips stained black in the limited light.

He looked up at Aung. "Dawn is coming. It will be difficult for me to get back to the troupe. Perhaps I should stay out here, listening?"

Aung smiled down at him. "A brave thing to offer, but I think not. There is too much risk of you being caught. Besides, there will be important discussions with the troupe. You may wish to be there."

As if anyone ever listened to him—but maybe they would if the old singer said they should.

"I will not ask you to return to your wood, but perhaps you could *pretend* you are wood and I will carry you. Does that work?"

Yamin considered, for being in-his-wood was never his favorite thing. But *pretending* he was wood— well, that sounded interesting at least.

"All right," he said gamely. "For the chance to get my puppeteer back." He raised his arms and Aung lifted him up and cradled him as if he was a babe in arms and then struck out across the clearing. "I'm not a baby, you know," he whispered at the old man's gentleness.

"And I'm not a ruffian. You are a valued puppet. Now hush."

Yamin held himself still, his eyes wide open, trying to scan everything and everyone without shifting his eyes.

There were even more people than he'd seen from the pinnacle the day before, as if they had multiplied during the night. They lay about the clearing like shoals of teak leaves along the river's shores, but these were all clogging the bright grass of the clearing and the entryway to the serpent stairs that led up to the abode of Min Mahagiri.

He really should sneak away and climb the stairs to meet the great man. Would Min Mahagiri welcome brethren? Surely he would be more welcoming than the other yoke thei who claimed Yamin was no more than a pest.

Overlooked and misjudged, that was his fate—except perhaps by the old singer. He sighed and caught a quick warning tightening of the singer's fingers.

Right.

He was pretending he was wood.

A huddle of men sat around a brazier cooking river fish brought up from the plain. There was something familiar about two of the figures. Perhaps it was the twist of their turbans, or the cut of their pasos, but something wasn't quite right.

"Sss," he hissed. "The men over there. Something about them."

The singer gave him a cross look, but followed the twitch of Yamin's finger in the men's direction. Pretending he was wood was one thing, but when a clue called, you couldn't simply ignore it, could you?

The old singer's gaze seemed to slip right past the men, but his stride shortened and he slowed. His gaze slipped back toward the men and held for a moment. Yamin felt the old singer's muscles tighten and then he hurried to the puppet enclosure. He ducked inside the curtain and almost collapsed until Saya Lin caught his arm and supported him to his stool.

Yamin leapt down to face him. "Did you see? Did you see them?"

"Be quiet, Yamin," Saya Lin said. "Can't you see Aung is close to fainting?" He called to the other puppeteers and musicians. "Bring tea. Bring rice. What has happened, old friend?"

Saya Lin knelt and helped steady the singer's shaking hands and Yamin placed a hand on the singer's knee. It was thin and sharp and boney as if all the bark had worn away. Almost like a dead tree.

Something aching and heavy clogged Yamin's heart. The singer was old, yes, but not so old yet, surely. They were just getting to know each other. Just getting to the fun things they would do together.

"Are you unwell, friend?" he asked.

The old singer shook his head, but his shoulders slumped. "Just fatigued, little friend. It has been a long night."

But surely fatigue alone did not justify the resignation he showed.

The singer turned his weary gaze on Saya Lin. "I fear that the king's men have come after us. Yamin spotted them. At least two, but disguised as commoners. One had a wicked scar that had taken off half his ear. What they could not disguise was their swagger, the length of their turban cloth, and the fineness of their pasos. The villagers might not have noticed, but I did."

The troupe master sagged. The old singer shook his head. "The king has declared a war upon the nats. Banning their worship. Chipping their likenesses from temples. What better way to end their worship than to destroy the greatest festival that celebrates their king?"

"Then to injure the nats, they might have killed the nat wife, Tet," Yamin said quietly.

§

Aung affectionately considered the little page. Yamin had transformed into a much more astute and thoughtful being. Yes, he was still willful and troublesome, but usually, to Yamin's mind, he had a very good reason for doing whatever he'd done. It was a side of Yamin no one had ever noticed before—at least no one ever remarked on it.

He nodded gravely down at Yamin. "That is well thought out. The question is, what do we do about it?"

Saya Lin shook his head. "We dare not do anything if it was them."

"What?!" Aung and Yamin said as one.

"But what of Thura and Zeya?" Aung added.

"Yes! What of my puppeteer? I will not lose him!" Yamin stomped his small foot.

Saya Lin held up his hands. "What would you have us do? Arrest King Bodawpaya's men? Take them as prisoners back to court? We barely escaped with our lives the last time!"

Aung looked away. It was true, as far as it went. Someone had murdered their Min puppet and that left the puppet troupe incomplete—unsuitable for a royal puppet troupe. So far they had hidden their deficit, but how long they could do so was anyone's guess. They hoped to be far from Bodawpaya and Amarapura, the capital, by the time it was discovered.

"Are you suggesting that we leave Thura and Zeya behind?" Aung asked.

"We may have to. There will be other boys to train." Though the words were harsh, there were tears in Saya Lin's eyes.

Dismayed, Aung had to catch himself before he fell of his stool. The dismay transformed to anger, fueling his strength. "Those are words I thought to never hear from you, old friend. We are a troupe. We are a family. The world is changing, I know. It may never see the like of this troupe again, but a true leader would never suggest such a thing." Aung wobbled to his feet and shook his head at his friend. "You make me ashamed. I will find a way to deal with this, if you will not."

He turned to Yamin, who actually looked frightened—something Aung had never thought to see on the face of the mischievous page. "I'll think of something, my little friend, but now I need a walk to clear my head."

He shoved out through the curtain and stood there inhaling the cool morning air and trying to still his roiling thoughts. Truly the world was changing, and not for the better. How could Saya Lin suggest such a thing? Thura was a son to Aung. He would not let him play scapegoat for the crowd.

The clearing below the pinnacle was filled with mist and slow-motion movement as the people roused to their day. Meat and rice cooked on small braziers and cook fires. People chatted companionably over their meals, but Aung did not feel part of it. His sense of dislocation was more than the wide space of empty ground left around the puppet stage and enclosure, and around the yellow awning. Even the gray-haired fortuneteller had apparently moved the longyi he had spread on the grass beside the puppeteer's enclosure the day before.

Though Aung raised his hand in greeting, the pilgrims who passed him carrying their offerings to Min Mahagiri rushed past to get to the stairs that began between the two white elephant statues. They pointedly avoided looking at him. He sighed. Perhaps it was his age that made him too old for all this change.

The crowd would coalesce soon and then they would demand Thura and Zeya receive swift justice. He glanced back at the yellow awning that held so many questions. Just as with the case of the Min's death, there were so many suspects: the musicians, the king's men, another nat wife, a lover.

He should have asked Yamin what the girl had looked like. Aung could look for her, then, but it was hard to remember everything that needed to be done when body and soul felt so exhausted.

With a sigh he went to find the wealthy man he'd spoken to last night to beg for more time.

The man had established an encampment just outside the pwe clearing in a secondary clearing just above the trail up the mountain. The place afforded a grand view of Min Mahagiri's pillar, given the clearing sat slightly higher on the mountain, so Aung could admire the white stone of the buildings and the golden glitter of the distant roofs that topped the massive stone outcrop.

The man sat, cross-legged in his plaid longyi, on a bamboo mat with three other men and a tray of laphet—pickled tea—and a bowl of steaming rice. As with many wealthy men, they discussed money, loans, and interest rates. By their fire, two women fussed with tea water. Though Aung had been unable to eat the food the puppeteers had brought him, he found his stomach growling at the nutty rice and the briny scent of the pickled tea.

He placed his hands palms-together even with his mouth and bowed respectful greeting to the man. "I bring greetings from our leader, Saya Lin, and pray that cooler heads prevail over the fates of our apprentices."

With a rice ball in his hand, the man motioned Aung to join them on the mat. His gray turban glowed golden in the morning light. "I am Zaw Htin and I organized the pwe and the nat wives who attended. These are my friends who have come from Yangoon to seek the blessings of the nats in a business venture."

He shook his head and filled a spoon with pickled tea, dried shrimp, and dried garlic. "But now, with what has happened, they will spend half their fortune simply to not have the ill luck of the pwe follow them home." He popped the spoon of laphet in his mouth and sighed. "And me? I may be doomed by this misfortune, for each year it is the nats' blessings for the festival that keep my family, my village, and myself healthy and prosperous."

Aung sat with them, though his old bones made it difficult to settle on the ground. He helped himself to a spoon of pickled tea and added chopped peanuts and shrimp, then enjoyed the pop of the briny flavor and the crunch between his meager teeth. It was his favorite food.

"I have spoken to the apprentices. They tell a tale of foolishness, but not murder." He recounted Thura and Zeya's tale. "You see? They are young, but there is no malice in them. Why would they kill a nat wife who they had never met?"

Zaw Htin arched a brow at him. "Why indeed. There are rumors that your troupe has lost the king's favor. Perhaps you have fallen on hard times? That could be incentive for a youngster to seek easy money. A successful nat wife would have had some wealth."

Aung bit back his shock at such a suggestion. He shook his head before the man could finish and set his laphet spoon aside, though the laphet was truly excellent. "We—things are different, that is true, but we have not fallen on hard times. We are a royal puppet troupe—the best in the land. We've just come from Bodawpaya's court, where we played for the royal wedding. Does that sound like we are in difficulty? Besides, you underestimate the honor of both those youngsters."

Zaw Htin popped another rice ball in his mouth. "Youngsters who, by their own admission, tried to hide the truth. Why should the people believe their story?"

"Because it is the truth?" Aung said. "Because there are other things at play here and other culprits. I just need time to prove it. I need you to convince the villagers to give me the time to investigate the other suspects."

Zaw Htin straightened his back and motioned for the tea, with a cup for Aung. Aung accepted the cup from one of the women and sipped its warmth and felt his tired blood surge to life in his veins. To simply curl up and sleep would be a blessed boon, but that was not to be. Lives depended on him.

"Why would I? What is in it for me?" Zaw Htin asked as he sipped from a pale celadon green cup. "We benefit most by a quick resolution to this matter."

"But do you benefit if the wrong men pay the price? Surely it will only bring more ill-will from the nats if their wife's true killer does not pay the price? And both the apprentices are linked to the yoke thei— nats in and of themselves. Would convicting those youth not affront the nats even more?"

The man on Aung's right grunted. He was a skinny fellow with a blue turban, dressed more richly than Zaw Htin. The blue-turbaned man used a laphet spoon with pearls on the handle.

"There is truth in his words, Zaw Htin. The price must be paid by the right man. It is not just a matter of having offerings made. The right words must be said, the right offerings made. Have we not all said that? Is that not why we came in person? Is that not why these nat wives were arranged? Otherwise we could have simply sent an offering here. There is merit in our pilgrimage and in the pwe."

Aung nodded. "The nats have been affronted by wrong action. I cannot believe they will be honored by a second wrong action."

Zaw Htin eyed Aung and his companions and sighed. "Fine. I will do what I can to hold back the villagers."

Aung bowed his head in thanks. "Then I must ask for your assistance on another matter. Can you tell me who saw the youngsters running from the dead nat wife? I would like to talk to them about what they saw and who was in the area."

The four men looked at each other. Finally the blue-turbaned thin man pulled his legs under him and stood. "I will show you. I would have honest results to this enquiry, but I will be back to finish our discussions, Zaw Htin, so do not leave here." He helped Aung up and then respectfully bowed. "I am Bo Thawda."

Aung bowed in return, but before they left, Aung turned back to Zaw Htin. "You said that you organized the pwe and the nat wives who came here."

Zaw Htin nodded. "Others may attend, but I ensure that there are at least five reputable wives and enough food kiosks and so on. The fortunetellers and liquor sellers come anyway. And this year the puppet troupe appeared to be a boon." He shrugged. "It all draws in money, am I right, Bo Thawda?"

"So we will hope, with the nats permitting," the blue-turbaned man said.

"Tell me," Aung asked. "Was the dead man, Tet, one of those you arranged to attend?"

"He was," Zaw Htin said, his expression grim. "He was from Arakan. A dreadful place, I understand, but I thought it would be good to see the difference of a nat wife from those parts. I had heard he was beloved of the nats."

Aung nodded. "I saw him once and he was—extraordinary."

He excused himself and, together with Bo Thawda, returned to the main clearing. The sun, now higher, had burned the mist away and the nat wives were preparing to sing. Already the bottles of toddy wine were tipped back, the heady liquor burning down too many throats. Soon the drunken anger could return and it would make it that much more difficult to find the killers. It would also make it that much more likely the drunken villagers would take misplaced justice into their hands.

"Here," Bo Thawda said. He pointed at a group of men and women sitting under a tree at a tea stand across from the puppet stage. They were eating their morning meal, though the men were already drinking. "These folk. They accused your young puppeteers."

Bo Thawda and Aung approached the group and Bo Thawda introduced them and Aung's purpose.

"Why should we speak to him?" Their leader was a tall man with long arms and one cheek branded by some fire in his past. "He seeks only to prove we're liars."

Aung shook his head. "I do not dispute that you saw the two apprentices running away. They admit that much. What they do not admit is the murder itself. I wonder if you might turn your minds back to yesterday afternoon and think about what else you saw? Who else might have had the chance to do this thing?"

The leader frowned and looked at his friends. "What say you?"

There were slow nods. A shrug.

"As you can see, we are not keen."

Aung stepped in among them and settled to the ground. "I appreciate whatever help you might give. There are lives at stake."

He scanned the faces around him, wishing he had the luxury of speaking to each person on their own, for by such a process he would obtain a diversity of perspectives. By talking to them in a group, he would obtain only one—a consensus that might or might not be correct.

"I would ask you to think back to yesterday. Were you all here? Where were you seated? What were you talking about?"

The leader scowled and glanced toward the pwe. One of the nat wives called out to the spirits. "The singing is started. We want to offer ourselves to the nats."

So this conversation would be interrupted soon enough. "Will it not be a gift to the nats if we determine who the true killer is?"

There were a few murmurs of agreement and finally their leader sighed. "I am Zaya Zarni. Yesterday there were four of us seated at the restaurant table. I faced the nat wife's enclosure, with my friends Thuta and Yaza on either side of me. My daughter Thi Thiri San sat across from me. There were many people about, visiting the nat wives and meeting friends. That is all I remember."

He looked from face to face and nodded, and the others who had been with him nodded back. It described the scene Aung had seen when he left the enclosure as well. Except Yamin had warned him of a body.

"Tell me more about the singing and dancing." Hopefully it would jog their memory of who was around.

Zaya Zarni frowned. "I remember it was loud. All the nat wives were singing and their musicians were playing and each orchestra seemed to try to outdo the other to the point where we could not hear each other at our camp. We went to the restaurant, for it was quieter at this end of the festival."

Aung nodded. The man's statement confirmed Saya Lin's choice for the puppet stage.

"You were relieved that it was quieter and that you could speak with me," Thi Thiri San said, her gaze respectfully lowered. She was a doll-like girl with thin, black hair, graceful limbs, large eyes, and a perfect bow of a mouth. Thannaka paste whitened her cheeks and arms. "My father has not brought me to such a festival before. He wanted to make sure that I was not shocked by what I saw or felt." She raised a surprisingly coquettish gaze to Aung. "The spirits are strong in me."

So she might appear a doll, but throwing off social constraints during the pwe's wildness was a welcome opportunity.

"It seems odd to me that you sought a restaurant tea kiosk to speak to each other and yet that tea shop is almost right across from two nat wife enclosures. Surely they were as loud as the others."

"That is the thing." Zaya Zarni leaned forward. "Though there was loud music from the blue and white enclosure, there was no one there at the yellow awning. No musicians and no nat wife. I put it down to him being Arakanese. Those foreigners do not do things as we do." He frowned, stretching the scarred skin of his face in shiny distaste. "But it is odd. The rumors said that his great voice would cause all the nats to abandon the other nat wives. I thought perhaps he showed compassion for the other wives and held off performing..."

That did not quite accord with the nat wife Aung remembered. The young wife he recalled had already been boastful and full of himself. If Tet had boasted of his prowess, had the other nat wives feared him? Was his threat enough for one of them to kill him? And where were Tet's musicians?

He looked back at Zaya Zarni and his friends. "Did you happen to see the dead nat wife before he died? Did you see his musicians?"

Zaya Zarni shook his head, but Aung stopped him.

"Please. Think hard. Each of you. Did you see the nat wife and his musicians when they arrived?"

The men all shook their heads, but the girl turned thoughtful. "When we first arrived yesterday—remember by the upper road? There were those men who looked like they had lost something. They kept looking back as if they had forgotten something. Remember? They were with that man who was arguing so publicly with a girl. It was as if they had no *bhamma-san chin*—no Burmeseness." She shook her head disapprovingly.

For most people, saving face by not showing extreme negative emotion was very important. For Thi Thiri San to recall such a display, the display must have been very bad indeed. Aung leaned forward.

"Do you recall what they were arguing about?" he asked.

"It was something about leaving, if I recall," Zaya Zarni said. "He wished to leave and for her to go, too. She wished to stay, so he left her here."

"And was there anything else about these men to suggest that they were musicians?" Aung asked.

Thi Thiri San thought for a moment. "It was more like it was the whole picture of them together. Two were large, like those who must carry the gong or drum circles. There were others, not so large but with the strong arms of a drummer, and there were two who were finely built—as if they played the hne. Do you understand? They all had the dusty, faded clothing that comes with much travel. It was one of the finely built men who argued with the girl. She was reed thin, too, so perhaps he was her brother? Her father?"

"Can you describe the girl for me?" Aung asked.

Thi Thiri San pursed her lips. "There was nothing special about her. Long dark hair. Large eyes. A small nose. She wore a faded paso that was somehow strange. Not flowers but fish were its design and she wore a blue blouse, I think."

It was as good a description as he was likely going to get.

"And have you seen any of these people since then?" He looked from face to face. Zaya Zarni shook his head. Thi Thiri San considered, but it was the man called Yaza, who sported a scraggly beard and a plain grey shirt and plaid paso, who nodded.

"Not the men, no. But I think I may have seen the girl late last night. She was in the crowd that came for your puppeteers. Do you think she is the culprit?"

"It is too soon to tell," Aung shook his head. "The girl. This man she fought with. There are too many suspects at the moment."

Around them the shadows had shrunk to midday and the nat wives' musicians filled the air with their wild music. Threading through them were the nat wives' voices calling on the people, calling on the nats, calling on them both to join in the dance to replenish the land and keep Burma and its people safe.

But this was just a mild buildup to what would happen when evening fell. Dusk would fill the pwe with drunken wildness. And in the dark there was no safety at all.

Chapter 7

The afternoon stretched as Yamin paced beside his wicker trunk. Perhaps it was because he was small, and when you were small and very long-lived, even time seemed to weigh too much. Or perhaps it was the puppeteers and musicians who lay about like lumps—even the one that the old singer seemed to consider his leader and friend. It was as if all the life had gone out of them, and even the yoke thei had mostly taken to their trunks where they returned to their wood, allowing their spirits to escape to the cloud fields of the north. Which left him with no one to talk to, no one to entertain, and too many worries for his small brain.

At least that was what it felt like. His head felt full. His chest felt hollow. First Zeya got taken and then the old singer became, well, old. Far older than Yamin had initially thought. As old as trees that collapsed in the forest, all their roots and limbs riddled by rot.

There was no way such an old man could be expected to complete the investigation, and yet Yamin—the old singer's chief help—was stuck here because of the sunshine.

There was no help for it. The other puppeteers and musicians talked softly amongst themselves or lay sleeping on their bamboo mats. A tray of half-eaten laphet lay forgotten to one side. It might be possible to ask one of them to seek out the old singer and ensure that he was all right, but it was doubtful that anyone would listen to a simple page.

Yamin stretched and yawned as if he was tired. "I think I'll return to my wood now," he said. He waited until one of the puppeteers nodded in his direction and then clambered up the side of the trunk that sat atop other supplies. Inside the basket he crouched down and peeked over the top.

Not a soul was looking in his direction. He probably hadn't even needed to pretend to sleep. He waited what seemed a suitable time—long enough for a butterfly to bob and dip across the curtained enclosure—a positive lifetime. He did one last check of the puppeteers, but they now played a dice game, and he slipped up and over the rear of the basket and down under the puppet stage, then slipped sideways to peer out under the curtain.

Too many feet and too many longyi and paso hems passed by where he stood. There was no way he could leave right here, right now. He needed to get to the pinnacle and slip along its base until he came to the rocks or the trees. Then he could keep to the edge of the forest while he searched for the girl he had seen. So far the old singer had not seemed that interested in her, but there was something going on, and didn't the solution of a mystery require the investigator to look at all possible solutions?

Maybe the old singer had forgotten that. He *was* old. It was a sad reminder that things were changing. Very sad, indeed.

Yamin eased along the edge of the curtain to the very edge of the stack of boxes and wicker baskets and peeked around the edge of the last box. The puppeteers were busy with their game. Perhaps they would not notice him when they thought him asleep.

He remained amongst the folds of the curtain and crept sideways, finally ducking out of the curtain when he thought he'd gone far enough. He came out where yesterday the fortuneteller had been, but there was no cloth spread on the ground now. Past a few rocks, the golden awning still stood abandoned.

Yamin scurried back to the tall grass and brush at the pinnacle base and paused. There was no outcry, so no one had seen him. Good. Now he just needed to follow the edge of the clearing and keep watching for clues—and the girl. He burrowed through the tall grass and bushes to the rear of the yellow awning, intent on reaching the rocky edge of the clearing.

"Clean this all up. The flowers are wilted and can be thrown away. Or wait, they are not so bad. Offer them for sale. The pilgrims are so drunk they may buy them to offer to the nats," said a voice from inside the yellow awning.

Yamin stopped dead. Were people supposed to be inside? Had the musicians returned? That would be news indeed!

A female voice agreed and Yamin frowned. To offer wilted flowers to the nats—that was courting trouble. In the puppet troupe, the puppeteers shared only the best with the yoke thei, for the puppets were the puppeteers' little brothers and sisters and should be honored. Their offerings to the nats when they performed were only the freshest of banana and coconut and rice newly made. Yamin bit his lip and leaned in. He did not like the owner of this male voice, whoever it belonged to.

"And have the awning pulled down. It is grand. The nat wife from Pyay has asked if he might buy it as it is much grander than his current one. I've set a good price for it."

The curtain rustled above Yamin's head as if someone jiggled it and he prepared to leap away in case the awning collapsed. Footsteps heading away said that wasn't going to happen—at least not yet.

"What of the nat figure? Shall we carry it up the pinnacle? Perhaps that is what is meant to happen. It could appease Min Mahagiri's displeasure," said the female voice.

There came a pause and then there were footsteps again. A sigh. "No... This we will need to carry home, I think. It is too valuable. Haven't you noticed the layers of gold leaf?"

"But..."

"No 'but.' That is how it will be. See it is done. We cannot leave this structure standing here as reminder to the crowd of what has happened. There is already enough undercurrent of violence. I'll not have more killing."

Two sets of footfalls walked away and Yamin hurriedly pulled up the curtain edge to see who the speakers had been. Min Mahagiri's elephant pedestal blocked his view.

He shoved past the elephant and strained to see. Too late—whoever it had been had disappeared into the crowd. He stood there, disappointed. A clue?

More likely someone cleaning up the killer's mess. He'd wasted precious time.

The sun was hot on his shoulders and head as he shoved through the grasses, clambered over rocks, and finally reached the trees. Beyond the rocks the land had fallen away in great layers of smoky blue on blue. He had never realized the human world was so big. It seemed to go on forever like unfolding blue cloth until it melted into the sky.

It could make one feel very small and he needed no reminders. The trees gave a welcome reprieve from the sun and the view, though the trees reminded him of his size, too. He quickly traced the edge of the clearing, checking through a screen of sweet-scented leaves to try to spot the girl he'd seen. The earth was comfortingly loamy underfoot, but the incense and brazier smoke masked the jungle's clean scent. The way the blue smoke hung in the air made it hard to distinguish human faces.

That and the fact that there were so very many humans. They all looked mightily alike. From his angle near the ground, they all had dusty, bare feet and dusty hems. They were all taller than him, all were too loud and uncaring in how they interacted with the world—crushing small insects and plants underfoot, scaring the birds, cooking their meat. For a moment he wasn't sure whether he even *liked* humans. Except the puppeteers, of course, and his apprentice puppeteer, and the old singer most of all.

"Think, Yamin. Think. What did she look like?" How could he tell her apart from the others?

He settled on his haunches under a huge elephant ear leaf to consider.

She'd been swathed in darkness and separated from him by leaves so he didn't know her features, but she'd had long hair like lovely princess Minthamee. He twitched a leaf aside to assess whether that would help him identify her. There was a girl with long dark hair coiled up behind her head. And there another. And another. And another.

He sighed and let the leaf fall back into place. So much for long hair as a clue. What else had he noticed about her? He scratched an itch at the base of his left ponytail. She'd been young. He was sure of that, because otherwise he'd have dubbed her a woman and first impressions were always important. But there were lots of unlined faces at the pwe festival.

So what else? Humans might look the same, but they differentiated themselves by what they wore.

That was it. She'd worn a blue top and her longyi had been faded but decorated with flower and fish images! That was surely unique. How many women wore fishes in these parts? He couldn't recall ever seeing one—not that he paid particular attention to the dress of human females.

He might have to start doing so...

Leaving the elephant ear leaf, he kept to the shadows to skirt the edge of the clearing. The afternoon was passing and the over-sweet scent of toddy wine filled the air. In the past, he'd seen the puppeteers fall down a time or two when they'd drunk too much of the wine. Now men and women staggered around the clearing or took up the jugs of wine that the nat wives offered. The songs of the nat wives rose in competing wails that felt like they could lift the skin right off his shoulders, the puppet strings pulled so tight. Here and there a spirit wife danced and was joined by villagers who seemed entranced into dipping and swaying in mirror to the nat wife's dance. But there were no girls with fishes on their clothing.

He was about to skirt a small side clearing to continue his search when something stopped him.

An old man and a young one occupied the small clearing. Indeed they seemed to have claimed it for their own, for they had a longyi spread upon the ground, its blue faded almost white, but across the faded cloth was a most unusual design of leaping dolphins carousing amid lotus blossoms. He stopped. A dolphin was almost a fish, wasn't it?

The old man had a sparse beard and thin hair much like the old singer, but this fellow did not wear a turban. Instead his wispy hair was tied up in a top knot. He also didn't wear a paso. Instead he wore thin white trousers and a long, white, high-collared shirt like the men from over the western mountains wore. The old singer wore such a shirt, too, different from other men. Hmm. Perhaps it was because they were both old? Yamin pondered that a moment. Was the clothing because they were old, or did the clothing make them old, similar to how a man could become almost holy by changing to a monk's robe?

The young man dressed as most men, in a plaid paso and vest over a bare chest. So these were ordinary people—except. The old man had small carved images of stone and bone in a carven gourd that he rattled and then spilled onto the ground. He studied the fallen items and then shook his head, then replaced them in the gourd and spilled them again. "Not good," he muttered. "Not good at all."

He looked up at the young man. "Where is your sister?"

The young man looked up from where he hunkered beside a fire pit to light a small fire. "I sent her for water." He frowned and stood as the fire sputtered to life.

Yamin edged back. He was not partial to flame.

"She should be back by now," the young man said as he scanned the crowd. "There are so many already possessed it could be a challenge crossing the clearing." But as he spoke, his face hardened. "I'll go find her."

He left the old man to his trinkets. The old man watched the young one go and then looked from the display before him on the ground up to the top of Popa's pinnacle. He shook his head and then scooped the bones and stones once more into the carven gourd. More fish, these ones cunningly carved leaping out of waves, covered the gourd's surface. The old man rattled it and mumbled a prayer before tossing the trinkets on the cloth before him.

"Not good. Not good," he said again and looked back at the pinnacle. "Min Mahagiri spare us all, please."

A chill ran up Yamin's back. This was a fortuneteller. He'd seen their like when he'd snuck out at other pwe, but usually they told happy tales of marriages to come and children born and healthy. This one was entirely distraught at whatever signs he read in his bones and rocks.

The light gradually fell and the noise from the pwe increased. Three drunken friends stumbled into the fortuneteller's clearing and collapsed in front of him, demanding in a drunken slur to know their future. The old man scratched his beard and demanded coin. It exchanged hands and then the fortuneteller rattled his bones and strange rocks with holes before handing the gourd to a disheveled youngster with smooth skin and a brown turban with the end of the cloth coil poked up as a display. The youngster impatiently rattled the bones and spilled them on the cloth between himself and the old man.

The fortuneteller hunched over the display, tracing a gnarled finger over the stones and bones. The men laughed with each other, but a stillness settled over the old man as if he stepped outside of this existence.

Yamin shivered and looked over his shoulder. The light was failing and there were nats about, he could feel it in the tingling in his wood. He fully expecting to see the Taw Saun—the guardian spirit of the forest— pick his way through the trees toward them. There was nothing there.

"Well? What does it mean, old man?" the tufted turban's owner asked.

The old man peered at him. "There are men held here against their will and they are favored of the nats. They are innocent. You must see to their safety or karma will not be good to you and all manner of ill things shall befall you."

The man's eyes widened. "But I've got nothing to do with them. No power over these people."

The old man sat up and the air around him appeared to glow. "You have a voice. Help them or let your doom befall you."

The old man sagged and the three drunks staggered up and back from him, then rushed back to the crowd. The two men could only be the two apprentices. So the nats truly tried to help them.

"Thank you, Min Mahagiri. We really do hold you in greatest esteem." Yamin bowed in the pinnacle's direction with his palms together at the crown of his head.

When he looked back to the fortuneteller, the fortuneteller's young companion had returned, dragging a girl with a bucket on her head. He shoved her forward so that water sloshed over her clothing.

"I found her halfway down the mountain," The young man spat into the dusty soil.

"And I told you that the line at the spring nearer the clearing was too long and the water had gone murky. I wanted clear water for father." She set down her burden and knelt to hug the old man. "I would not leave you, father."

"So she says now," the young man said and shook his head, then went back to stab the sputtering fire.

The girl smiled at the fortuneteller, her blue blouse bright in the remaining sunlight, her longyi in smooth folds around her, the fish in the design leaping over lotus blossoms.

It was the girl! It was as if great Min Mahagiri had conspired to bring him here! Yamin leapt up and his movement sent the bushes rustling. The fortuneteller and his kin turned toward him.

Yamin froze. He eased a step back. Another.

"Is someone there?" the old man asked, his voice trembling.

"There are small creatures about in a jungle like this," the girl said, but she scanned the jungle just the same.

Small creature, indeed. Yamin swallowed his pride and slowly backed away, then hurried along the jungle's edge. In the clearing the light was fading, the falling sun painting the smoke and the shifting bodies red. The singing had increased in volume as the villagers took up the nat wives' songs. He needed to get back to the puppet troupe's enclosure. He needed to find the old singer and tell him what he'd found.

§

Within the puppet troupe's enclosure, a debate raged. Over the course of the afternoon, Saya Lin had become determined that they could not afford to wait much longer before leaving. The soldiers that had been spotted could take word back to the king. There could be repercussions to the troupe simply for coming here. They needed to leave now and put many more miles between themselves and the city of Amarapura.

Saya Lin had presented his decision to Aung upon Aung's return, though the other puppeteers did not seem so keen. Saya Lin's adamancy just made Aung tired. So did the fall of the sun. Another day gone and the apprentices were still held in the monastery cell; the puppeteers had brought them a tiffen of food to share, but his chest was filled with the sickness of failure. This had been a great puppet troupe—the greatest the kingdom had ever seen— and now they were to be reduced to squabbling refugees who would abandon their brethren?

He shifted on his stool and wished Thura was there. The lad could massage his tired feet and legs.

Where were the clues he needed to solve this thing? He and Bo Thawda had spent the afternoon searching for the girl described by Zaya Zarni and his friends, but there'd been no sign of a girl with fish on her longyi. Such was a design he had seen in the south, in Arakan, but never so far north. Was this the same girl whom Yamin had professed to see? Surely it must mean something that both she and the dead nat wife were from Arakan.

So many questions and so many motives for death to take the nat wife—love or hate or politics.

He shook his head. The breeze seemed to pick up. The curtain trembled, but then Yamin tumbled in from the direction of the pinnacle.

"I found her! The girl!" The little page stumbled up to Aung, his face bright with excitement.

"The girl? Where?"Aung struggled to his feet.

Yamin frowned up at him with his hands on his hips. "What? No reprimand for being out alone during the day? I, for one, was very careful not to be seen." He waggled his ponytails proudly.

Aung glanced at Saya Lin's less than happy face as Yamin's entrance interrupted a terse discussion between the troupe leader and the musicians. Aung nodded down at the little puppet. "It was very bad of you to disobey. Thank the nats, you weren't seen." Aung glanced at Saya Lin again, but the troupe leader's anger really didn't matter anymore. "So? Where is she?"

The little page clearly enjoyed the way the puppeteers and musicians gathered to hear what he said. He paused, picked a grass seed from his pantaloons and then looked innocently up at Aung.

"Well?" Saya Lin exploded. "Are you going to keep us guessing, infernal page?"

Yamin huffed a sigh and lifted his chin. "That was not kindly said—at all."

"Yamin," Aung gently caught the page's shoulder. "This not the time for suspenseful theatrics. Perhaps you should just tell us."

Yamin cast a scowl at Saya Lin and then looked brightly up at Aung. "Of course. Most reasonable. She is the fortuneteller's daughter. You remember the old astrologer who had a blanket spread between our stage and the yellow enclosure? They have shifted spots to beyond the nat singers in a small clearing at the edge of the jungle."

Aung looked to the sky. The light was fading, the sky turning slowly from blue to golden as the sun descended. Beyond the curtains, the wailing voices seemed to come from everywhere as if every Burmese spirit walked here and had taken up residence in a body. At nightfall it would get worse with all of society's rules and customs fallen away. Anything could happen when the wildness set in.

"I have to find her."

"I will come, too," Yamin said.

"No, you will not!" Saya Lin said. "You will go safely to your basket where we can take care of you."

"I will not!" Yamin stomped his foot. "I am not a boy to be ordered around. In fact, I am far older than you—than anyone here! My apprentice is in danger and I want him back."

The enclosure went silent. Saya Lin had to shake the shock out of his gaze. Never in Aung's long life had he seen the page be so—well—pointed and not foolish at all.

"I can carry you as I did the other day if you will lead me to her," Aung said.

Yamin held up his arms and Aung picked him up so that Yamin could see, even when he feigned wood.

"I'm sorry, Saya Lin," Aung apologized. "I know you try to do what is best for the troupe, but abandoning our apprentices is not the way."

"Yet exposing our Yamin is." Saya Lin shook his head and sighed. "I never would have foreseen this discord between us, old friend. How are we to heal this rift?"

"Let me bring the youngsters back and all will be as it should." Without waiting for a response, Aung stepped beyond the curtain.

The jungle surrounding the pinnacle oozed darkness into the clearing. As the light failed, the glare of campfires and smoky torches became angry eyes between the staggering press of people. As soon as Aung stepped away from the curtain, people jostled his shoulders. He almost dropped Yamin and, as he crossed the clearing and the press of people increased, he was almost knocked off his feet a dozen times, the last by a turbaned man with a horrible scar that had taken half the man's ear. He was drunk and reeling, and the light in his eyes spoke of nat possession.

Aung froze, but the man staggered away, dancing. One of the king's soldiers, but clearly he was here as part of the celebration. A wave of relief swept over Aung. The king had not sent the men. They had come on their own to seek the nats' favor. The sweet scent of toddy and the lightly narcotic betel filled the clearing along with the sweat of men and women. At the nat wives' awnings, open spaces were filled with more people swooping and twirling as the nats shook them loose in their bodies.

He edged farther from the dancing and soon found himself up against the edge of the jungle. "I got Zaw Htin to promise that he would not let Thura and Zeya be taken by the crowd this night. But we need to find who did this before the pwe ends. Otherwise the crowd may demand to take them into Kyaukpadaung to hand over to the authorities." Kyaukpadaung was the nearest town—a large one with a military presence.

Yamin stirred in his arms. His fingers squeezed Aung's arm. "There."

Ahead, the trees around the clearing parted as if to create an anteroom to the larger space. There a cloth was spread upon the ground and a young man guarded the entrance. An old man sat cross-legged in the center of the cloth with a fortuneteller's charts and paraphernalia spread around him. There was no sign of a girl.

"She was here," Yamin said. "I saw her."

"Shh. Let me see about this."

He shoved through the last of the press of people until he reached the young man, who leaned against a tree.

"What do you want?" the young man asked, straightening to confront Aung.

Aung drew himself up to his most important and squared his shoulders. "I am here about the girl. Perhaps she is your sister? I am Aung, Master Singer of the royal puppet troupe. I need to talk with her on a matter of some importance."

"There's no girl here. Go away." The young man said.

Aung met the sad gaze of the old fortuneteller. He nodded and the old man on the cloth nodded back. "Then perhaps I'll consult with the fortuneteller to find out what I need to know."

For a moment it looked as if the young man would block his way, but then he shook his head. "Fine. Spend your money."

Aung settled himself before the fortuneteller, laying Yamin across his lap. Thankfully, Yamin remained still—to the point that Aung began to wonder whether the little page had actually returned to his wood.

"I am here on a matter most urgent." He introduced himself. "Yesterday two apprentices from my troupe were wrongly accused of murdering the nat wife. I am trying to uncover who committed this horrible deed. At the time of the death, a girl was seen near the place the nat wife's body was found. I am told that same girl was seen with you. Can you tell me where she is? I must speak with her."

The old fortuneteller stayed silent, only the slow rise and fall of his chest and the pwe torchlight shifting in his eyes proving that he lived. They were shuttered eyes as if he looked not without, but within, and Aung recognized a man bent on contemplation. This was what his life would become when he left the troupe for the monastery.

"I told you," the young man said. "There is no girl for you to find."

But the old man's breathing quickened.

"Please. Surely the spirits do not approve of innocents being killed and a guilty party going free."

The fortuneteller's gaze went black, all reflection of torches washed away. "You walk with the nats and have for many years," he said. "They are always near to you." His gaze flickered down to Yamin and his hand stirred across his lap to touch Yamin's foot.

The page quivered but stayed still.

"There is no peace for you. You have travelled long roads, but will travel many more and some will bring danger to you and your kin. I do not understand it, but it is your fate to have a kinship with wood." He bowed his head. "Sometimes you cannot save someone from themselves."

When the old fortuneteller looked up again, the strange darkness in his gaze was replaced with something else. Did the he speak of Aung or himself? A foretelling of this kind was not helping him catch a killer.

"And the girl?" he asked.

"There are events swirling about Min Mahagiri's home. Who can say where a lone girl rests?"

Aung leaned forward. "Please. There are good young men's lives dependent on catching the killer."

The fortuneteller's throat worked and he seemed to sag into himself. "My daughter is a gentle soul. She would not kill anyone, least of all a nat wife."

Aung thought of the grief Yamin had seen—not the usual emotion of a killer. Remorse, perhaps, but not simple grief. "I believe you, but she may have seen something. Please tell me where she is and I will go to her."

Looking out to the shifting figures of the pwe, the old fortuneteller nodded. "She prays with the body."

Of course she was with the body. It made sense, given her grief. Yamin cradled in one arm, Aung lurched to his feet and bowed to the fortuneteller. "Thank you. I will remember you in my prayers."

Aung nodded at the angry young man, but the youngster turned away. Sighing, Aung turned to the pwe where the night had fallen, turning the clearing into a place of wild, shifting shadows and light. Glimpsed faces in ecstasy or in tears. The possessed whirling in place and tearing at their clothes. The nat wives staggering around their musicians, calling down the nats and further inciting the people. It was no wonder Saya Lin wanted to get the troupe off the mountain.

He paused at the edge of the melee and the young man left his post by the trees and came toward Aung, his expression threatening. Aung hurried into the crowd, but glanced behind him. The young man's hard gaze followed him.

Why was the young man so angry?

Though the spirits were abroad this night, it was unlikely that the body would be displayed in the clearing. There was too much chance its presence would incite further violence. Given the nat wife had no family here to care for it, it was most likely that it would be at the monastery either on the top of the pinnacle or on the mountainside where Thura and Zeya were held.

The crowd was too thick and too rough for him and he nearly fell too many times—for these drunken fools had little capacity to even notice an old man in their midst. Instead they swore at him when he got in their way. Finally, he took to the trees, only to trip over couples copulating just inside the jungle edge.

"Put me down," Yamin whispered. "Put me down and I will lead you. I remember that your eyes are not so good."

It was true. With age came so many indignities that he could not care for himself as he once had. At times it was as if life prepared him for the death that was to come, stealing away everything he had been able to do for himself until, finally, in the end, he would be left with nothing and someone else would pray for him.

Someone else would gain merit on his behalf so that he might return to a better life.

And if he were alone, as the nat wife had been? It was strange that the musicians had not stayed with him. True friends and family—and after so many years, who was Aung's family but his troupe? Would it not be the same for Tet, the nat wife? What had frightened his family away?

He settled Yamin on the ground where the little page straightened his clothes and peered up at him. "That young man was most unpleasant."

"Yes. Yes, he was, but perhaps he had a reason," Aung said.

"The fortuneteller was not so bad." Yamin considered. Then he grinned. "Your fate entwined with wood, indeed!"

He reached up and caught Aung's hand and led him through the trees. "We're going to the monastery, aren't we? That is where humans take bodies, is it not?"

"Most insightful, Master Page. Now just where did you learn that? Have you made a study of humans?"

Yamin shook his head, his ponytails bobbing bits of greater darkness. "Perhaps you've rubbed off on me, singer. I see the need to know about them if I'm to catch a killer."

Never would Aung have expected to hear such a thing from the foolish joker, Yamin. He grinned into the dark. "You've grown, Yamin. Truly grown."

Grown enough that he now provided the ears and eyes that Aung seemed to have lost over the years.

For a moment, to prove it was not so, he almost let go of Yamin's hand.

Chapter 8

The monastery gate loomed large in the moonlight. Thin wisps of cloud spun away from the mountaintop to cling around Mount Popa's pinnacle and turn the almost full moon nacreous blue. The light placed shifting leaf shadows under the trees and over the stout wooden gates of the monastery. Vines wound up the walls, their blooms tightly closed against the night, but their sweetness remained, combined with the incense that came from beyond the gate. Two figures were carved into the stone on either side of the gate, the brother and sister Mahagiri nats who ruled over the mountain.

Yamin released the old singer's hand. "You go ahead. I will wait here—though I want to know everything the girl says."

He read the doubt in the singer's gaze. "Truly. There is too good a chance of me being seen, though perhaps I might visit Thura and Zeya. They are likely lonely and wondering if we have forgotten them."

The old singer considered him and then nodded. "I will trust you to do this and I will meet you there, but be careful, Yamin. I would truly hate to lose you."

Yamin watched the old man hobble through the gate. He would hate to lose the singer, too. He remained where he was, listening to the distant music of the nat wives. He was getting rather tired of the noise. That was likely why there was only one large festival a year at the mountain—it was all Min Mahagiri and his sister could abide. At the moment, the main ceremony was happening at the temple on top of the pinnacle. A chosen nat wife would call down the spirits and their blessings.

From the jungle came the cracking of a twig that spoke of animals abroad in the night. He sighed. Better to be small and inconspicuous in the abodes of men than to be eaten in the jungle. He stepped up to the gate and peered inside.

Master Aung was just disappearing into a small building on the far side of the monastery. The sound of low chanting came from that direction. Voices came from the larger mediation hall; and across the swept grounds of the monastery and the grove of banana palms and hanging laundry, the cell that held the two young humans held a candle glow.

A Death in Passing

He stepped through the gate and edged his way around the wall.

§

The body of Tet, the nat wife, lay wrapped in strips of unadorned, undyed cloth on a raised wooden platform in the middle of the small teak-walled chamber. It was not a rich room as one might find in city temples complete with golden Buddhas and golden draperies. Instead a white stone Buddha with orange-painted, sequined robes reclined as Buddha had done before he died. Around him was a pantheon of the thirty-seven nats, each clothed in their appropriate colors and with ornate robes and crowns. Offerings of fruit and rice lay in low wood bowls around them and bright flowers garlanded the necks of every one, but their sweetness could not mask the sickly sweet of death.

Beside the dead man, a young woman knelt with her head to the ground, her arms outstretched in prostration. Between her outstretched hands a single stick of incense burned, smoke coiling upward toward the blue cloud that clotted the ceiling. From beneath the fall of hair, her whispered prayer echoed around the room like ghostly voices while from some hidden chamber came the low reverberation of monks chanting. The fact they did not chant around the body spoke volumes, for the dead usually received monk's prayers and teachings to help guide them from this life

111

to the next. But Tet was the victim of violent death and not even the monks liked to be near such a body. The victim of a violent death was usually cremated almost immediately, lest their angry ghost begin to haunt the world. Such a dead person would not believe that they were dead and could become a hungry ghost.

Aung stood at the door, taking it all in. He did not want to interrupt such fervent prayer, but he truly needed to talk to the girl. The fact that she was here confirmed Yamin's story. The fact that the body was still here suggested that she had somehow influenced the monks.

He cleared his throat to let her know of his presence.

"I told you! I will say the prayers if you will not." Her voice was choked and tearful. "I will not let you just get rid of him. He was a good man. He will be reborn as a good man again." Her voice caught again.

"I believe you," Aung said and stepped inside the room beside her.

The girl jerked upright, palming tears off of her face. "Who are you? What do you want?"

Aung settled cross-legged to the floor beside her. He introduced himself. "I seek to learn who killed this good man so that I may save the lives of two other good young men. I hoped you might have information to help me."

He sat there patiently as she considered him. Her gaze was heavy on his skin as if she read him.

"How do we know that you speak the truth? There are those who would hide it." Her voice had changed, becoming deeper and manly. The girl's gaze went blacker than her father's had.

For a moment Aung did not know what to say. Then he understood. "You—you are also a nat wife."

"I was. I am. This body serves me sometimes, though it is not supposed to." Then the girl shuddered and suddenly she was herself again. She shoved her hair behind her shoulders and gazed at him defiantly.

"So. What will you do with this knowledge?"

Aung cocked his head. "What could I do with it? It is a fact. Is it to be hidden?"

"My brother and father would say so." She shook her head. "The spirits have walked with me all my life, though my father refuses to acknowledge it, and my brother despises it. I am to make a good marriage instead. That is what they want for me. Not to become as those you see at the pwe."

Her words were bitter, but she looked up at him with such tragic eyes that he had to look away. Such tears were foreign to *bhammasan chin*—Burmeseness.

"And you wish to dance with the spirits?" he asked mildly.

"That and other things," she said, openly weeping. "There are so many endings."

Aung reached for her hand as a grandfather would. "Tell me. Tell me your name and what has happened."

She looked at him, her gaze dull, though her eyes reflected the candles. "What good will it do? Tet is dead."

"It may save two innocent men. Would that not earn merit for Tet's reincarnation?"

She looked away to the shrines, the gleaming benign faces of the nats and the dying Buddha.

"My name is Mya. My father is Lwin Naing and my brother is Kywe Myint. We traveled here from Arakan, far in the south, for my father wished to show me the truth of the nat wives. He wanted to show me what I would become and hoped that it would disabuse me of my determination."

She sniffed and straightened, her face hardening as she wiped her tears away.

"It did not work, of course, for I wanted to come. I knew Tet would be here. If father hadn't come, I would have left to follow Tet myself." Her gaze softened as she raised her gaze to the body. "He was a good man."

"And you loved him," Aung said softly.

Her gaze jerked back to him. "Does that shock you? That a woman would love a spirit wife? I knew Tet long before the spirit took him. We were in love and then it happened—spirits came into both our lives. He was older. He left our village and found another nat wife to learn from. I was younger and a girl, so I stayed home, but always I waited for him, hiding what I was— until my brother found out. He demanded that I marry, but I said I already was. Father was unhappy. And then Tet came back to our village, by now a mighty nat wife on his own."

She looked to her free hand in her lap. "I ran to him and threw my arms around him. He held me and then he held me away. We could not marry, he said, but I did not care. I wanted to be with him. I would follow him anywhere."

"So you came here. What happened the day of Tet's death?" Aung asked.

She shook her head, her eyes filling again. "I don't know. It was horrible. I came to his tent and there was so much blood. His musicians found me there, with the body, praying that it was not so—he could not be dead. The night before, I had told my family my decision to leave them and travel with him as an apprentice." She shook her head again. "So many plans broken."

"The musicians dragged me with them to leave the pwe, for Tet's spirit would be angry at dying and there could be much ill-luck befalling those who remained with him. There was one among the musicians who had spoken to my father about a marriage to me, but I refused him. He tried to force me off the mountain, but I would not go."

Aung nodded and the room was filled with the low chants of the monks praying Tet through the place between this life and the next. Hopefully convincing Tet's spirit that he was dead so that he would leave peacefully. "That was the altercation that was seen by the road."

She nodded.

"So what happened afterward?"

"I went to return to Tet, but there were people there. I hid, for I was afraid of being blamed for his death. I went with those who sought the killers. I was there when they caught your friends. I—I am sorry."

She bowed her head and Aung sat back, feeling lost. Her story was a sad one, but it made sense. The trouble was, it did not point the finger at a single killer.

"Who do you think might have killed him?" Aung asked.

"I don't know." She covered her face with her hands. "I've wracked my brain, but I do not know. My father. My brother. Htut of the musicians because he wanted to marry me?"

"So you think them likely suspects, too?"

"As likely as myself, for I was discovered with Tet's body just as your young men were."

Except only the musicians had seen her and they were not here to testify about it. "Do you truly think your father and brother capable of killing Tet?"

She thought a moment. "My father would not have the strength. This journey north was hard on him. My brother, though—he was so angry when I told them what my plans were. He called me all kinds of names and would have little to do with me until my father reprimanded him."

That was something—an angry brother could be capable of killing.

"What will you do now?" he asked.

She smiled. "I don't know. I pray for guidance that I may do what is right to help Tet to a good life."

"Would you be willing to tell your story to the pwe patron? It may change his mind about the two young men he holds and help him see their innocence."

She swallowed and nodded.

And so he left her.

Outside the chamber the night was cool, but the scent of incense was strong. Soon the scent of cremation would fill the air, for it was not good to keep the body of one who died a violent death for even the traditional three to seven days. It was a marvel the girl had managed to hold off the monks and the villagers as long as she had for the man she had loved.

Love was a strong motive.

The gritty soil crunched underfoot as he crossed to Thura and Zeya's chamber. He found them huddled around a single candle, finishing off the last of the food that the puppeteers had brought that morning.

"Have you brought more?" Thura asked, looking up hopefully.

"Is food all you think about, lad? Your life is in play here."

"I, for one, think they are entirely not worrying

enough," Yamin said, stepping from behind Zeya. "They smile entirely too readily."

"Is this true?" Aung asked, settling himself on the floor, though Thura leapt up to aid him down.

The two young men looked at each other. "We worry, but there isn't much we can do about it, and we have you working for us. What more could we hope for?" Thura said stoutly.

"And me. You have me, too!" Yamin said.

"They most certainly do and he has been a most able investigator. There is only one challenge. The clues we have gathered all seem to lead to a dead end. The girl we sought is here, but her story only widens the net of possible suspects and if we cannot produce the culprit— well, there is no telling what the people may do."

All the concerns he had managed to keep at bay descended on Aung's shoulders and he closed his eyes. He felt sick and weak and hopeless, but he could not let the young men see his despair. It was Yamin who laid a hand on his knee.

"It will be fine, singer. We will think of something. We will." His little face held such determination that Aung had to smile.

"With such certainty, surely the clues will come our way." He explained what the girl had said. "It seems to me that our likely killers are either the would-be lover who left with the musicians, or the brother who did not approve of Mya's decisions. When I saw him and the father, the old man seemed resigned, but the brother was angry."

"Anger can lead to violence, so the ancient stories say," Yamin agreed.

"Then I dare not stay here. I must find the brother and confront him," Aung said and clambered to his feet again. He held out his arms so Yamin clambered up like a child in a wizened tree and then assumed his pretend wooden form. Aung said goodbye to the apprentices and took his leave. At least they were well so far. Zaw Htin had held the villagers off, but he would not be able to forever. There were too many possible evils afoot as long as the killer was uncaught and unpunished. With the nats receiving such negative emanations, it was more likely that they would send ill luck to those who had come to the mountain to gain the nats' favor. It would take many offerings, or a resolution of the case, to undo such a state.

He kept to the jungle, threading through the dimly lit paths with Yamin's help. Along the way they found more couples copulating in the jungle, groups of men drinking and singing at the edge of the clearing, including Zaw Htin, his eyes glittering in the light from his fire as he surveyed the event he had sponsored.

The page gripped Aung's hand and acted as his eyes, leading him around the people, so he had nary a misstep along the way. Finally they reached the small bay in the clearing. The old man sat cross-legged on his cloth as if he was a Buddha statue touching the earth. Only his eyes flickered as they caught the torchlight from the pwe. Overhead the moon was full and fat and pouring forth a pearly light. Beyond it, stars glittered dimly, their light shamed by the orb.

Aung motioned Yamin to stay where he was and stepped up beside the fortuneteller. "It is the final night, but who knows if this wildness will give the nats what they want. I personally think not, for the nats are capricious, but lovers of justice. Too many nats died through past unjust practices." He stood above the fortuneteller.

"You think I do not know that? Can you not feel the anger in the air? It is not just these fools resenting the extra offerings they must make. It is the very air itself and the earth underfoot, the forest trees, the creatures. They all resent what has happened and demand it be put right." The fortuneteller looked up at Aung, his dark eyes filled with the moon's light so they glowed fiercely strange. "I should have never come here, but I was so certain of the future I had read. It said that my daughter would marry well. I did not believe it would be to a spirit. I saw death and thought it the death of her ambitions, but who am I but a father and a foolish old man."

He looked back at the pwe and the bawdy actions of the men and women. "Do you have children?" he asked.

Aung shook his head. "I have an apprentice. I am trying to save him."

The old fortuneteller nodded. "It is a father's role to save them from themselves."

"Sometimes you can't." And sometimes you must let them feel the pain of their actions, but please Min Mahagiri, let it not be the beheader's blade. "I need to speak to your son."

"You can't," the fortuneteller said. "He left not too long after your visit and went to climb to Min Mahagiri to seek a blessing for our journey home and for his sister."

"What do you know of the dead man?" Aung asked.

"He's dead."

"I understand that you knew him. That there was a relationship between him and your daughter."

"Yes. Yes." The fortuneteller glanced at him, his sharp gaze catching the moonlight. "The foolish girl said she loved him and at the same time claimed to be wed to a spirit."

"So you did not agree with her."

The old man shook his head. "What father agrees when his child seeks disaster? It is not so much that she wished to wed, nor that she wished to become a spirit wife—but both together? And now Tet's death has sent her farther from me than ever." He sighed. "Would that Tet had not died. At least he would have protected her, for he loved her in his own way."

Aung sorted through what he'd been told. "So you had come to accept her decision?"

The old man hung his head. "I had come to accept that we all have our own path to walk and that though I may see it, I cannot control the future."

There was such hopelessness in the fortuneteller's voice that Aung wanted to comfort him, but suffering was part of life and it seemed that old man had brought it on himself.

"Who do you think killed Tet?" Aung asked gently.

His sharp gaze was back and held on Aung. "You are the one asking questions. I thought you would know by now."

The wind brought the tinkle of small bells even over the noise of the pwe. Aung lifted his gaze to the top of the pinnacle where the temples would have bells hanging at their corners. It was a long, arduous climb up seven hundred and seventy-seven stairs. Somewhere there trod his prime suspect, for the old fortuneteller might not have the strength, but his son certainly did.

The moonlight glimmered on the gilt rooftops and on the roof of the stairs coiled round the pinnacle. Did Aung even have the strength to make the climb, let alone confront the young man?

"It seems that I must at least try to talk to your son. I leave you now to your meditations." He backed away into the forest.

"Meditations, bah," the fortuneteller snorted. "I get pleasure out of watching all these upstanding men and women make fools of themselves. Tomorrow will see such remorse."

Aung looked back out at the crowd caught in the frenzied outpouring of emotion and lust.

Remorse? No. The pwe was about releasing what you were capable of—all the things proper society denied you, not about finding shame.

He stepped amid the trees and the jungle rose around him. Yamin appeared through the bushes.

"Give me your hand, and I will guide you."

Aung did as requested and the little page looked up at Aung. "So what do you think? Did the brother do it?"

Aung sighed. "I cannot say without speaking to him, but each man or woman who came here brought their own hell or heaven with them. Those who bowed to the greatest controls in their lives were likely to dive deepest into the nat's dark pool of release. And those without the deep control, those who pandered to their emotions and needs, are most likely to engage in killing. Whoever killed Tet is probably not lost in the wildness of the pwe."

Yamin looked thoughtful. "Such a man might climb the pinnacle instead of enjoying the pwe."

"For such a one, the pwe offers nothing. They already give into deep emotion."

"We must find him, then." Yamin nodded and began to lead him through the jungle and hopefully toward a solution.

Chapter 9

The puppet troupe's stage and their enclosure stood next to the stairs that led to the pinnacle, but Yamin, in his efforts to be unseen, had always left the enclosure on the other side away from the stairs. Now he sat in the singer's arms and looked up in amazement. Two life-sized white elephants of stone flanked the night-darkened entrance to the stairs that gaped like a mouth ready to swallow the clearing.

He looked up at Aung. "I do not like its look, singer. All those stairs and a possible killer to push you down them."

"We do not know he is the killer."

"But he is our suspect."

"We've told Saya Lin where we are going. That is all we can do. Now hush."

Knees and hips popping, the old singer laboriously climbed the stairs toward the mouth that awaited between the elephants.

"You sound like a poorly made puppet whose joints are failing," Yamin whispered.

"And you sound like a naughty young page who does not know how to talk to your betters. Now hush."

Yamin harrumphed and lay back in the singer's arms. This was no way to climb the stairs—as a burden, a piece of cartage.

They reached the elephants and stepped between them under the stairway roof. During the day the ornately tiled ceiling probably kept off the worst of the sun's rays, but now, though they were open to the pinnacle's stone on one side and the countryside on the other, the roof only held in the remains of the day's heat. The air was still, but filled with whispers.

Yamin sat up. "Do you hear them? There are spirits here. Nats and hungry ghosts, I think."

The old singer had stopped and was listening. "There are voices, but I cannot make out what they say. Can you?"

The voices were like feathers that touched the skin and lifted away so you could not be sure they had ever been. They were a hush as if leaves blew across stones, but there was nothing distinct about them. Yamin shook his head. "They are watching us. They know why you are here, but I don't get the sense they agree with it."

He frowned. "Put me down, please. There are enough shadows that I can hide well enough. Perhaps I can hear more if I don't have to listen to your old man's breathing. Has anyone ever told you that you wheeze like a bellows?" He grinned up at the old man and the singer set him on the stair.

Soon they were climbing together, for no one seemed to want to climb the stairs and chance missing the pwe.

"What happens if we miss the brother?" Yamin asked as the stairs rose up the pinnacle's side. Already they were above the pwe, so below them stretched the fire-lit clearing and the sea of dancing, figures. The wild music soared up to their perch and, beyond the clearing, the night-darkened folds of Mount Popa's jungles fell away toward the distant, moonlit plains of Pagan. He clambered up on a windowsill and waited for the old man to catch his breath.

"I suppose we return to his father and await his return."

Yamin studied his old friend. "Perhaps we should do that now. Your face is red and your wheeze has become the sound of a most angry wind in the trees. You do not look well and I do not think these stairs are for you."

But the old man shook his head. "It must be done." He grabbed hold of the post that held up the ceiling and trudged up another few steps.

Yamin leapt down from his perch and scampered ahead of the old singer. His old friend looked close to collapse. Perhaps he could run ahead and find the brother, then return and tell the singer to wait. In fact, given there was no other way off the pinnacle, why not simply wait at the bottom of the stairs? But knowing the stubbornness of the old singer, Yamin had best be able to report on the current location of the brother.

He rushed up the stairs, all seven hundred and seventy-seven of them, and stepped out onto white paved stone amongst buildings perched amid the rough white stone of the top of the pillar. The spirit voices were louder here, though the wind blew through the buildings as if they were deserted. The small bells high on the steeply pitched golden roofs set off ting-ting-tinging like a small creature's heartbeat.

Yamin stood in the darkness seeking a sound that would tell him where the brother had gone. No sound. No one, and yet he knew he was being watched. He hurried across the pavement, his feet making less sound than a leaf would. This high up the air was cool, the breeze new and crisp, catching in the bells on the eaves and his ponytails. The door to a temple yawned open and he ducked inside. Surely the brother would be here, praying.

The room was empty, the floor cold stone. On one wall a row of niches stood complete with statues of the thirty-seven nats with Min Mahagiri and his sister. Beside them was Mi Wunna, the beautiful, flower-eating ogress who fell in love with Byatta, an official of the king. Byatta had been tasked with gathering flowers from the mountain, but then he met Mi Wunna and fell in love. He failed to bring back the flowers and the king had him killed for it and kidnapped Mi Wunna as well as Mi Wunna and Byatta's two sons. Mi Wunna died of a broken heart and joined Byatta as a nat. Their sons died, too, at the hands of the king, and became the Taungbyon brother nats. So much violence and sadness these nats had seen. No wonder the humans were afraid of them. They had much to atone for.

All of the figures were garlanded with flowers, but only a single incense stick trailed smoke in front of them.

Yamin frowned. That was strange. If all the people dancing in the clearing were here to make offerings to the nats, their offerings should be piled high on the floor. Was this another mystery?

For a moment his heart quickened and he wanted to dash off to find the culprit, but there were bigger questions this night.

"No, you shall be like the singer and be single-minded of purpose tonight." He nodded and turned to leave, but the sound of soft footsteps stopped him.

He scurried into a corner and crouched, as silent and still as a shadow in the darkness.

A man stepped into the temple. He was tall and straight-backed with the broad shoulders and strong arms of a mighty man. He had dark hair twisted in a topknot and dark eyes so piercing Yamin cowered back, for this was no ordinary human.

He wore only a simple paso and a vest that exposed a broad, smooth chest of golden skin. A twist of red cloth bound his handsome brow. With him came a breeze scented of cinders and frangipani.

He stopped by the door, scanned the room, and frowned. "I know you are here, little man. I smell you."

Yamin started from his crouch and smelled his armpit. "I do not smell!"

He revealed himself, stepping out to confront the stranger. "I bathe regularly. The puppeteers make sure of it!"

The man's frown transformed into a smile and his strange black eyes glowed deepest amber as if a flame was banked deep inside. He was most certainly the kind of person one did not want angry.

Yamin pasted on his most innocent expression. "How did you even know I was here? I am very small and very stealthy."

The man nodded. "You surely are. And a very good investigator, or so I've heard."

"You have?" Yamin stepped a little closer. "Really? I have only been involved in one investigation. Well, two if you count this one." He shook his head. "This one really is most puzzling."

The man peered past him into the shadows of the room and his face grew troubled. "This is a holy time. A time for man and spirit to become one. A time for blessings, but someone has turned it into a travesty."

As he spoke the man's voice got louder and he increased in size until his head reached the ceiling. His huge, blackened hands made fists. Not a man! A nat! Yamin fell back and then he fell on his knees, realizing who stood before him.

"My Lord, Min Mahagiri," Yamin said, his forehead pressed to the floor. "I did not realize. I am sorry for my affront to you."

The great man chuckled. "Stand up, Yamin, smallest of the small and yet great of heart and mind. You have done nothing to abuse me. In fact, your plots amuse me most of the time."

Yamin looked up. "They do? Princess Minthamee says I can be very tiresome. Even the Master Singer says she has a point."

"Ahh, but they have to live with your pranks every day. I do not."

Yamin scrambled up. "So you mean that there is moderation and I should practice it. I have been trying, you know."

"I know, Yamin. And I know that your mind has not been on jokes while you have been investigating. Have a care that you don't change too much. Don't forget why children love you. But that is not why I come to you this evening."

Yamin looked up at the great nat. Min Mahagiri knew everything. He could tell who the killer was.

"You've come here seeking someone, but you will find he has no answers."

"From what we know, he's the one who was angry enough to kill the nat wife. Certainly it was not the young singer or my puppeteer."

"It was not." Min Mahagiri agreed and slowly shrank back to man size. "They have been raised around the nats. They know our might and capriciousness."

"Cap—riciousness?" Yamin frowned at the new word.

Min Mahagiri leaned down until his face was next to Yamin, his breath like a mixture of lemongrass and toddy wine. "Capriciousness is like you, Yamin. One moment full of helpfulness and the next the bane of someone's existence. Your killer has forgotten that fact. There is more than love and anger that lead to killing, little page. Remember that. Did not your old singer say that there are those who do not abide by customs and so they do not need the pwe to show their true selves? Violence comes easily to such people and for colder reasons than anger." He motioned toward the other nat figures. "Many of us were killed by such men. Without prayers to help him, your dead nat wife may yet become a nat."

Yamin's mind whirled with this new information. He blinked up at the king of nats, trying to make sense of it all. "Why not tell me who murdered the nat wife and let us deal with it?"

The great nat threw back his head and laughed. "Because I am a nat. Because I am capricious."

The earth shook underfoot, and the temple bells jangled. The incense stick fell over onto the tiles and the smoke ceased coiling. A stiff breeze blew through the door and Min Mahagiri came apart and swirled away like ash.

"Capricious, indeed. I think you're a show-off," Yamin mumbled as he brushed dust off his clothing and left for the stairs. The old singer wasn't going to like this.

The wind fluted through the buildings with a sound like laughter.

§

The pinnacle shook under Aung. He sat on a stair where fatigue had finally forced him to give up his quest to climb the mountain. Beside him in a pool of moonlight, one of the water pots intended for the pilgrims pitched over, but no water spilled out. Odd, when it was important to always keep them filled. It was an honorable task that the pilgrims expected. The quake sent the pinnacle monkeys screaming, awakened from their dreams in the trees. By the electric feel of the air, something had disturbed the nats and he could imagine a small puppet who might have something to do with it.

Please do not harm him. He has grown dear to me.

He sent the thoughts spinning out in a prayer

and was surprised to realize that he meant it. Both Yamin and Thura were like sons to him.

And he was old and hopeless and mostly useless, for how was he a help to anyone, let alone Thura and Zeya, when he could not even climb a few stairs? When he had to depend on Yamin to do his work for him?

The barest of breezes found him. He was just so—tired. More so because of this investigation—what if it was not the brother? What if he had become too single-minded and the killer was actually one of the other nat wives? Or the soldiers, as he'd first suspected? Even if the brother *could* be the killer. He had the opportunity and motive, but there was something niggling. Something in what the old fortuneteller had said to him and for the life of him, he could not recall what it was. That was the problem with age—it ate the memory, too.

The sound of footfall above him brought him struggling to his feet. He held onto the nearest roof pillar to steady himself as a man-sized figure appeared out of the darkness.

"Who—who's there?" he asked.

The figure stepped down a few more steps until, by the moonlight through the open side of the stairs, Aung could make out Mya's brother, Kywe Myint. Aung looked past him for Yamin, but there was no sign of the page. Had something happened to the little one?

He looked up at Kywe Myint and read the anger still burning in the young man's gaze.

"What are you doing here?"Kywe Myint asked.

The fact he asked gave hope that Yamin had not revealed himself.

"Actually, I am waiting for you. Your father said you would be here."

Kywe Myint looked up and down the stair. "This seems an odd place. You chose to climb half way up the pinnacle?"

Aung sighed. "No, I intended to climb the whole way, but it seems old legs can betray one's desires. I wanted to talk to you about your sister and the dead nat wife."

The young man closed his eyes and sighed. "That man seems to haunt me. When I close my eyes, I see him looking back at me. His death causes Mya so much pain and I would not wish that for her." He shook his head and sank down on a step, nodding for Aung to join him. "What can I tell you?"

"Tell me about what happened."

"What happened?" Kywe Myint looked surprised. "I thought you knew. Mya loved Tet, but he would not marry her. He broke her heart, and I wanted her to abandon those dreams and marry another—a good man. She refused, and against my better judgment, I agreed with father to come here, to let her see how she could never be Tet's wife. How hard it would be to be a nat wife herself." He shook his head. "And then he went and got himself killed and all of my father's foretelling spoke of dark things. We had come here, hoping to make a profit with my father's work, but instead we needed to make more offerings. We were going to leave here poorer than when we arrived—and for what? My only sister devastated and determined more than ever to become a nat wife? It has been a disaster!"

He covered his face with his hands, and his shoulders shook. "Your pardon, please. It is this place. These times." He quickly wiped his cheeks and composed himself. "What more do you need?"

"Did you kill Tet?" Aung asked softly.

"By all the spirits and the king of heaven, no! To kill a nat wife and bring the nats down upon us all? Never!"

By the fear in his eyes, Aung believed him. Raised with a fortuneteller, this one would believe in spirits, which meant he was unlikely to chance angering them.

And that left Aung's investigation exactly nowhere.

He bowed his head. "Thank you for answering my questions truthfully."

Kywe Myint stood. "In truth, it was good to talk with you." He looked up the stairs. "I just gave Min Mahagiri the last of our money for his blessings. Hopefully we can earn our way home." He reached for the gourd dipper beside the pot of water.

"It is empty. No one has filled it."

Sighing, Kywe Myint set down the pitcher. "That is what this pwe is like. So many of the things that should be done, are not. With the money offered to the nats, there should be golden dippers to drink from."

Shaking his head, he left Aung behind and disappeared down the stairs.

Chapter 10

"You got your wish, I see." Yamin stepped out of the shadows and into the moonlight spilling through the open side of the stairs beside the old singer. The countryside beyond the stairs was filled with a fine silver glow and he felt the quiver in the air of the nats' power.

He tugged on the old man's paso. "Do you feel it? The nats? They're all around us. They must have brought the brother to you."

"Shh, Yamin. I am having a thought."

By the look of the old man's face, it was a very deep one. His brow was furrowed. Deep frown lines pulled down the sides of his mouth.

Yamin tapped his toe while he waited for the old singer's thought to finish. By all the nats in Burma, he had so much to tell the singer if he was only prepared to listen. Time was ticking away and perhaps the true killer was getting away. The wild pwe music still continued, though, which suggested that he might still be around. Even if, as the old singer said, the killer didn't believe in the nats, he would still want to fit in.

Finally the old singer heaved in a huge breath and looked around as if he did not remember where he was. Then he spotted Yamin and his gaze cleared.

"Master Page, have you been all the way to the top and back? What have you learned, if anything? I fear I may have sent you on a wild goose chase."

The old man sank down to sit onto the stair again as if anything else was beyond him.

"You look tired, singer," Yamin said and settled beside the old man's knee. A metallic scent came off the old man's skin as if an unpleasant fire dwelt within.

The singer nodded. "I swear my very soul is weary, Yamin. These dangers to our troupe members wear on me and I fear that I do not have the strength I once had to solve the problem."

Yamin thought about that. "But you solved the mystery in Amarapura and saved all of our lives. How is that a failure?"

"I did not save everyone and deaths weigh heavy on me. I suppose it's because I can see my own ahead." The old man shook his head.

Yamin stood to face the singer. "And now who's speaking foolishly? It certainly is not the page. You have many years ahead of you yet. Good years because I, for one, will make sure of it." He brightened. "I will keep you young with my jokes!"

"Buddha preserve me from such help!" But at least the singer was smiling.

Yamin nodded and seated himself, satisfied that he'd brought a smile to his friend's face.

"So what did I learn at the top of the pinnacle. I did climb the whole way and it was very long. I do not think you would have made it." He covered his mouth. It was a stupid thing to say when the singer was already feeling old. "At the top there was no one around to see or see me. I went into one of the temples there, the one with all the nats." He scratched the base of a ponytail and thought. "It was very strange. For all this is a festival and many offerings are made, there were only flowers there and a single stick of incense like one might see at an almost forgotten shrine."

The old singer looked thoughtful again, and Yamin rushed on for he did not want to wait to tell his story.

"While I was there, a man came in and talked to me—except it was not a man." He leapt up again and danced about. "Can you guess who it was? I'll bet you can't!" He stuck out his tongue at the singer, but the singer seemed preoccupied.

"It was Min Mahagiri, singer! The great Lord of the Mountain, himself. He strolled right in as if he owned the place. I suppose in a way he does."

But the singer appeared less than impressed. In fact his gaze seemed far away.

Then he shuddered, bolted to his feet, and stood swaying.

"By all the nats and the King of Heaven I've been going about this investigation all wrong! I've focused on who would want to kill the nat wife, when that is not the answer at all!" He looked wildly down at Yamin. "Do you understand, Yamin? We've been thinking this whole thing has to do with the girl and Tet when it has nothing to do with them at all!"

Yamin rolled his eyes heavenward. "That's what I've been trying to tell you! When I was in the temple up above, Min Mahagiri came to me. He told me that there are reasons beyond love and anger for one to kill. He repeated to me what you said before—that there are those who do not need the pwe to show their hidden selves. That violence comes easily to those people for colder reasons."

The old singer nodded and a frown filled his face. For the first time Yamin could remember, the old singer was angry.

§

Aung spat and felt suddenly cold.

Around him the staircase filled with noise: the voices and music from the pwe, and a whistling roar from the top of the pinnacle. The air turned thick and hard to breathe. The silver moonlight blinded his eyes. He gasped and his knees began to buckle, but something unseen caught his elbow and held. New warmth and energy flowed into his limbs. His legs strengthened. So did his resolve.

He straightened. "No offerings before the nats because they've all been taken. No water in the pilgrim urns because people must be paid to fill them. What does that sound like, Yamin?"

He looked down at the page and the little one's mouth hung open in awe. "Did you see? Did you hear them? The nats go before us down to the pwe. They are with us!"

"Against injustice." Aung nodded. "Perhaps there is yet hope for our apprentices."

They hurried down the stairs through the darkness, and if anything, the music turning wilder, the shouts and shrieks louder. At the elephant statues that guarded the stair entrance, Aung stopped.

At the base of the stairs, the clearing was a mass of churning people. Like shifting islands, here and there, those taken by the nats dipped and bowed and whirled in place, like fish caught in the net of the nat wives' voices. The people were in a state where it would not take much to turn them into a mob that could force Zaw Htin and the monastery to hand over Thura and Zeya. If what Kywe Myint had said was true about the costs increasing in order to gain the nat's favor, there must be great frustration brewing and great anger. The lads could be slaughtered if no one protected them.

"Singer?" Yamin's bright voice and the tug on his paso hem brought him back from his dire thoughts.

"Yes, Yamin?"

"I was thinking—I heard someone in the dead nat singer's compound. They were talking about selling the musical instruments and the awning—for a good price, too. The golden Min Mahagiri effigy, they at first said they were going to remove to the shrine on the pinnacle, but then one of them said that they would keep it themselves. It certainly was not at the shrine above."

"The things will need getting rid of," Aung said. "They were worth a great deal, I'm sure."

"But if the statue isn't in the temple, it must be with the culprit." The little page looked up at him. "I, for one, think it is a clue."

"You could be right," Aung said, thinking about it. "You're certain it wasn't up there? It could be some place other than the temple."

Yamin shook his head, his ponytails bobbing. "Before I came down, I looked around the buildings. That was the only place it could have been."

"Then that is very strange indeed. Perhaps it is still under Tet's awning and has not been moved."

"It was a very valuable statue," Yamin said.

Aung thought of the many layers of gold leaf that had covered the surface, enough to make the effigy very precious. "Yes. It was. It may not be quite the Mahamuni Buddha, but its gold alone could feed many families for a long time."

He picked Yamin up and went down the last stairs to the curtained puppet enclosure, then paused and went around it to the golden awning.

The effigy wasn't there. Neither were the musical instruments, nor any of Tet's offerings.

Silently, he left the golden awning and ducked through the curtain and into the midst of the puppeteers and musicians. "We have a problem," he said to Saya Lin. "But I believe that I know how to fix it."

Chapter 11

With Yamin still in his arms, for the little page deserved to see this thing through to the end, Aung led the puppeteers and musicians through the rowdy crowd to the old fortuneteller's space. The old man still sat cross-legged on the spread cloth, but his astrologer's charts and his gourd of stones and bones had been packed away. At their small campfire, Kywe Myint crouched to nurse a pot of rice over the coals. Beyond him, the jungle was a dark wall, its noises overwhelmed by the cacophony of the pwe.

"What do you want?" said Kywe Myint as he stood to face them. "Will you arrest me even though I told you the truth and would not kill the nat wife?"

Aung shook his head. "I know you spoke the truth. I thought, instead, that you might wish to be with us when we confront the culprit. You sister, too, for that matter."

"You know who killed Tet?" Kywe Myint asked.

"Of course he does." The old fortuneteller's voice cut through the noise. "Did I not tell you that this one is different? His relationship with the wood helps him befriend the nats."

The old man's secret smile said he knew far more than he was telling.

"Go get your sister, she will want to be there."

Kywe Myint hesitated, but then left them to cut through the trees toward the monastery. Beyond the fortuneteller, the size of their gathering had caught the interest of those near them. Word was spreading that the puppet troupe's singer was to confront the true killer.

When Kywe Myint returned with Mya, the fortuneteller's blanket had become the eye of a growing crowd that had diffused into the jungle in order to hear what was said. Little was, for Aung feared the crowd would act without confirming the truth. There was too much chance of the crowd of revelers becoming a mob.

He and Saya Lin led through the crowd, with Kywe Myint and Mya behind them while the old fortuneteller remained behind. He already knew the truth, he said.

They cut through the thickest part of the pwe

and headed up the trail to a clearing by the road. The moonlight was fading toward a nascent dawn, so the eastern sky aspired to color. The pinnacle was a fading silhouette in the darkness, and the golden roofs at its top caught the last of the moon and starlight. Below them, the pwe was a shifting cauldron of humanity and firelight. The seething mass was somehow appropriate given Mount Popa itself was a volcano. Yes, the power of the people could overwhelm whoever had killed the nat wife, just as the mountain's shuddering could throw down entire villages.

Two fires lit the clearing, one small where the women labored over tea. The other fire provided warmth and light to the four men who held vigil around it. Aung nodded to Saya Lin and the puppeteers melted away into the forest around the clearing. The musicians and the fortuneteller's children stayed with Aung.

"Master Singer!" Zaw Htin smiled up at him. "We have spent the night sending prayers to the nats for the gift of good luck in the coming year. I included you and your troupe in my prayers."

Aung half-bowed with his hands palm together by his face. "And I thank you for your prayers on behalf of all of us. I'm sure it was meant as a kindness."

"What brings you here so early on this morning?" Zaw Htin asked.

If he understood what was about to happen, he gave no sign.

"I come because I have discovered the true killer of Tet the nat wife." Aung stepped forward and the crowd stepped forward with him. At last Zaya Htin's brow rose as if he suddenly registered that it was the villagers who swelled the size of Aung's puppet troupe.

"Yes?" Around Zaw Htin, the other merchants looked puzzled. Bo Thawda of the blue turban frowned.

"Let me tell you a story," Aung began. "Once there was a wealthy man, who the nats had blessed to gain his great wealth. The trouble was, the man forgot where the good fortune came from. Because he did not care for the nats and make regular offerings, the nat's blessing dwindled and so did the man's fortune."

"Yes. Yes." Zaw Htin waved the story away. "My friends and I are just about to have breakfast. They are leaving before sunrise, now that they have finished propitiating the nats. It has been a good festival, though it had a difficult start."

Around him the other merchants nodded, though Bo Thawda of the blue turban looked troubled.

"Why tell us this story?" Bo Thawda asked.

"All stories are either great legends like the Ramayana, or they are teaching tales. Let us consider this a teaching tale. And I have not finished mine," Aung said.

"The man fell into great debt with his creditors and though he made offerings to the nats, his luck was gone. He decided that the nats did not exist and that all his past luck had been his own. He decided to create new luck by using the nats to help his cause. He took on the task of organizing a momentous nat festival, for it is tradition that the organizer will not only gain merit with the nats, but may access the gifts to the nats to cover their costs. And as the man no longer believed in the nats, how easy it was for him to simply take what was given."

The four merchants stirred uneasily, Zaw Htin most of all. "Enough of this," he said. "The rice is almost ready and there is not enough to feed you and your friends."

A disturbance in the jungle beyond the women's fire stopped all conversation. Saya Lin and the other puppeteers stepped from the trees carrying something they had wrapped in a golden cloth. Saya Lin nodded and a wind suddenly swirled around the clearing. Both fires sent up great gouts of sparks and sent the women and the merchants leaping back.

"What is happening?" Bo Thawda demanded.

Aung held up his hand. "Let me finish the story, for my friends have found the final answer.

"The trouble for our wealthy man was twofold. First, his creditors announced they were coming for the pwe, and he knew this meant that they wanted their money. Second, the people who come to the festival are often poor, and poor people do not have so much to give. To feed their children, they hold something back. He needed to break down this barrier. To do so, he came upon a plan that not only reached more deeply into the purses of the poor, but that would have the added benefit of robbing his creditors.

"You see the festival is all about gaining the nats' favor, but everyone knows that if something bad happens, the nats will be displeased and will require more offerings to simply remain in their good graces. Gaining good luck or benefits will demand even more. He only needed to cause the people to fear that the nats would bring bad luck. What could be worse than someone's death?

"So someone had to die—someone whose death would be momentous for all. Who better than the greatest nat wife of this generation?"

Zaw Htin leapt to his feet. "I will not allow this slanderous story to continue. I have done nothing wrong. Nothing! You have no proof at all!"

Aung shook his head sadly. "But that isn't so. Your avarice knows no bounds. You sold the musical instruments of the nat wife's musicians though they may yet return to claim them. You sold his awning. But you could not simply sell his shrine, nor could you bring yourself to donate it to the nats on the mountain as any normal man would do."

Aung motioned to Saya Lin and the puppeteers. They threaded through the crowded clearing to Aung's side and Saya Lin uncovered what they held: a battered wooden statue.

"It was found amongst the trees just yonder," he said and lifted his chin beyond the women's cooking fire.

Aung nodded for Saya Lin to hold up the statue for all to see. Gone were the rich gold and red clothing. Gone was the golden face. Instead, the face and shoulders were almost gone, its wood grain torn and gouged where someone had chipped off the layers of gold leaf. The thing lay lifeless and deformed in Saya Lin's hands and the wind gusted down off the mountain once more.

"This was Tet's effigy of Min Mahagiri. It was thick with gold the morning of his death, but you removed the statue when you sold the awning. A friend of mine heard you discuss placing the statue in Mount Popa's shrine, but then deciding to take it yourself. When he saw it wasn't on the mountain, I knew what had happened. You found the last, most offensive way to regain your wealth—kill a man and steal the offerings."

The wind off Min Mahagiri's pinnacle became a gale, tearing sparks from the fire, leaves from the trees. It ripped Aung's turban from his head. His thin gray hair caught in the wind. Behind him the crowd growled their anger. Mya screamed and leapt at Zaw Htin until her brother caught and held her. The three other merchants leapt to their feet, yelling questions at Zaw Htin, while down from the pinnacle came a clamoring sound of shrieks and howls.

"No! No! It is all lies," Zaw Htin shouted into the roar of the wind.

He shoved Bo Thawda away from him and the crowd surged forward. Zaw Htin turned and ran for the trees, even as the jungle thrashed as if the very mountain came for him.

Monkeys. The silver-gray beasts of the pinnacle swarmed through the trees. They bounded through the brush, converging on Zaw Htin. Yamin stiffened in Aung's arms.

One of the beasts dropped on Zaw Htin's shoulder. He screamed and tore it off. Two more leapt onto his back. A third found his head. Their long wiry arms wrapped around him. Teeth and claws ripped his skin. More of the beasts trapped his legs and he stumbled as he tried to rip away. Around Aung the wind roared but the crowd had gone strangely silent. The great nats would have their way.

With five of the beasts on his back and more swarming up his legs, Zaw Htin stumbled at the edge of the jungle. He went to his knees.

His screams joined the clamor of the nat wives' music as he tore futilely at his attackers. Then his voice became a liquid gurgle and the weight of the monkeys forced him down. For a moment he thrashed against them, but then his limbs were weighted down and there was only a keening.

Then all went silent. Zaw Htin. The monkeys. The wind.

Only the wail of the nat wives and the clash of the gong circles carried up from the pwe clearing. In silence the monkeys left their victim and, like silver wraiths, they filtered through the trees back toward Min Mahagiri's pinnacle.

"Hungry ghosts," Saya Lin whispered, and broke the spell of shock that held the clearing.

Aung looked down at Yamin.

In the coming dawn the page's eyes glittered roundly.

Chapter 12

The morning sky was blue and filled with fluffy white clouds that carried the little rains northward, but the puppet troupe's enclosure felt strange, even though Thura and Zeya were back among them. The puppeteers were too quiet and even the apprentices were subdued. The other yoke thei were consumed with their primping and preening.

Yamin watched them from his perch on his wicker basket and thunked his heels against the sides. Bored. Bored. Bored. If he was newly freed like Thura and Zeya, he would most certainly not be simply sitting eating breakfast, no matter how hardy. *He* would dance and sing and very probably play a couple of jokes. The old alchemist puppet was particularly fun to tease because he was so intensely—serious.

Hmm. Maybe he could start something now that the mystery was solved. It had been quite a horrendous ending—not that the culprit hadn't deserved it. And seeing the monkeys in action made him appreciate just how fortunate he had been that first morning. Of course, being chased by the monkeys had led to the body's discovery and a mystery to investigate.

Or perhaps it wasn't good fortune. He squinted up at the pinnacle, its green sides and white and gold temples at the top silhouetted against the blue. Had it been Min Mahagiri's plan all along?

He thought about it a moment. "Very clever," he said and nodded.

"What is so clever, master page?" The old singer sat on a stool not far away, a cup of green tea clasped in his hands as if he warmed them.

He looked tired today, but it was almost a good tired—as if a long labor had ended. Yamin jumped down from the trunk and plopped down crossed-leg in front of his friend.

"I was just thinking that this was all meant to be, singer. Min Mahagiri had his monkeys chase me just so that I would find the body and our investigation would ensue." He nodded. "It was very smart of him for we are very good at solving mysteries."

The old singer studied the contents of his cup. Then he poured its remains on the ground in a slop of leaves and brown water. It really was a most unappealing drink. Plain water would be much better for the roots of a man—or yoke thei.

"What would have happened if Min Mahagiri didn't dispatch his own justice when he set his monkeys on the rich man? Would the crowd have torn him apart due to our accusations?" All the lines on the singer's face seemed to deepen with worry and he looked up into the sky as if he thought of flying away.

Yamin scrambled up and caught one of the old singer's hands. Beyond, Thura had the puppeteers laughing at a humorous song he had composed about the trials of being a prisoner. Yamin could actually enjoy the words and simple tune because the nat wives' wild music had ended. The festival was over and beyond the curtained enclosure, the pilgrims were once more wrapping themselves in the propriety of their customs, all the wildness of the pwe locked away.

"What is it, old friend? Something troubles you?"

The old singer smiled down at him. "In truth?"

"Of course truth. I, for one, would never lie to a fellow investigator."

The old singer sighed. "I am very old, Yamin. I've told you so before. I am thinking that it may be my time to return to the monastery in my home village. I will not be in the way there. Thura can take up the songs and I will have—peace. The events of last night were very unsettling. To see a man half-eaten, half torn apart... because of what I said. It is a heavy responsibility."

"But you did not call the monkeys down."

"But it might not have been the monkeys. Don't you understand? Without the monkeys, the people were going to do the job. They were very angry because of what I said."

"The truth? Isn't that what you were seeking? Sometimes the truth is hard, singer."

The old singer was looking at his hands and his empty cup as if he was empty himself. But—but he could not leave. Where would be the adventure in a monastery? Long hours of boring contemplation—a mystery was much more fun!

He was just about to say so when a female voice called from beyond the curtain. Saya Lin stepped outside and then returned. His face was pale.

"It is that girl, Mya. She wishes to speak to the investigators. Plural. How can she know about..." He raised his chin at Yamin.

"She is a spirit wife herself, though only a fledgling one. Perhaps the spirits have told her. The little ones should return to their baskets. Yamin I will keep her here with me, but he will pretend he is in his wood, won't you, Yamin."

Yamin frowned. It really would be quite interesting to see the new spirit wife's reaction to him. "I would be most polite if I could be myself."

Saya Lin rolled his eyes, but the old singer smiled. "I know you would be, but your kind cannot be exposed."

It was just the type of kindliness that made the old singer so important. Yamin couldn't remember how he'd spent his days before they began to investigate mysteries and he could not imagine how it would be if the old man was not there.

Yamin sighed. "We will do it your way."

The other yoke thei were coaxed into their baskets and Yamin sat leaning back against the old singer's stool, inhaling the old man's comforting scent of betel.

§

The Mya who entered the puppet enclosure was not the grief ridden girl Aung had met beside Tet's body. Nor was she the furious banshee she had been when they confronted Zaw Htin. Though her hair was still dark, it was now coiled up behind her head in a matronly way. Her clothing was the same—a simple flower and fish motif on her longyi and a plain blue blouse that reached her waist, but her face was stern, her dark eyes gone darker that the night skies of Popa with a silvery sheen as if the moon shone within them. The nat was on her, then.

He struggled to stand, but she waved him back down. She placed her palms together at eye level and bowed to Aung. Saya Lin urged the puppeteers and musicians out beyond the curtain.

"You have no need to bow to me or this body this day, for I owe you a great debt for exposing the true killer. It is too often that they walk free and some innocent pays the price."

Her voice was a blend of a woman's music with a deep male voice layered underneath. Above her the fluffy clouds roiled together and became gray with blessed water.

Aung bowed his head. She had truly become a nat wife. "So you have made your choice to join the nats," he said.

"By finding the killer, you made it possible for Tet to pass on to his next life in peace. This body thanks you for that, but that is only one reason I am here."

Aung looked back to Mya. The morning sun sent a beam through the clouds that glinted on her hair. There was a shimmer around her as if a half-seen presence enveloped her.

"Who are you?" he asked.

"Who do you think?"

"You are Mya and someone else. Min Mahagiri?" Aung guessed, for he was the resident nat of this place.

Mya bowed. "I am both. And I wish to thank you and your accomplice for a most interesting investigation." She looked pointedly at Yamin. "It held me amused through most of it—until the ending, in fact. I barely had to feed you a clue."

Yamin was positively vibrating beside him. It was a wonder the page didn't leap right up. It was a sign of how much the little one had grown and changed in the course of the two investigations. So was the apparent concern Yamin had shown for a silly old man. "So that is why you spoke to my—accomplice."

"Of course. But the knowledge I gave only confirmed your direction."

Aung bowed before the great nat.

Mya was silent long enough that Aung looked up at her. She smiled sadly down at him. "You are a humble man and a wise one. It has come to my attention that you are considering retiring to a monastery, there to rest your mind in contemplation. Is this true?"

Aung nodded and looked away. The decision was made even though Yamin's bright gaze glittered up at him, beseeching him to say no. "It seems best for everyone. I am old and tired and becoming a burden. The world is changing and there is no place for an old fool like me." He looked back at Mya and Min Mahagiri. "I forced the troupe to come to Popa to perform for you and all I did was almost lose our hope and future. I could not even climb the stairs to your shrine to give thanks for the safety that you have given us."

Mya crouched down to him and looked him in the eye. "It seems you misjudge yourself, Singer, for you have done me a service that could not have been done by any puppet performance—not even by these most excellent nat-imbued yoke thei—yes, I recognize you watching me, Yamin. Now stop this pretending and talk with us."

Yamin leapt up and dusted off his pantaloons, then bowed most courteously to Mya, but then bobbed his head in Aung's direction. "Finally. He thought you might not know about me. He's always so worried about keeping me secret and doing what's right."

"And that makes him a very special fellow." Mya looked back at Aung with her moon-glow gaze. "That is, in fact, why I wished to speak with you. Yes, the world changes, but that means that the old ways and your knowledge are more precious, for the world will not see those like you again. As I said, bringing justice to my nat wife's killer was a great boon—greater than any puppet performance. The debt of your puppet troupe is paid. But I have a bargain for you. Are you interested?"

Aung hesitated. The bargains of nats always held peril in them, for they were very tricky creatures that were as quick to anger as to give. "What kind of bargain?"

"A simple one, really. There are many injustices in this land. The king grows old and madder by the day. His officials are corrupt and his people lose their way and forget the nats. Foreigners attempt to change our people. There is need of a man like you to right the wrongs that come from such situations. I would ask you to hold off on your plans to retire for a bit longer. Conduct these investigations on my behalf to help the people. At the end of a year, you can reconsider. And for my part, I will take the worst part of your aches and pains upon myself."

"Singer! That is a very fair deal! I, myself, would take it but it is not asked of me. Just think of the places we can go—of the adventures. Of the fun!"

Yamin's face shone up at him. Around him hung the puppet troupe's curtain with its bamboo mats and the wicker trunks that were everything that counted as home. Beyond the curtain, the voices of the puppeteers spoke of years of camaraderie. Thura might be ready to sing. They might not need him, but someone did.

"Please???" Yamin's plea was unheard of. The yoke thei rarely said please and the little page never had in Aung's recollection.

Aung looked at Mya and decided, for truly he would miss his comrades. "If Yamin can say please, then surely I can do this thing, but I make no guarantees that we will solve your mysteries. There are too many vagaries in the world and too many people who do not want mysteries solved, nor the old ways held to."

"Then so it shall be recorded. I accept your accord." Mya stood and winced as if her bones ached. "For one year you will seek out mysteries and I will wear the worst of your age." She nodded once and stepped toward the curtain.

Aung shifted his stance and was surprised that his hips and back did not protest. Could it be true? Had the nat truly relieved him of the worst of his age? For a moment he felt giddy at this wondrous turn of events. Then guilt settled in. Why was he worthy of such a gift when so many others like Saya Lin experienced age's pains? This—this was a boon that required serious payment.

"Where should we go next?" Aung asked.

"Yes, where? I, for one, would like to know where we are headed, for the rainy season is ahead and I do not like to get rain on my paint," Yamin said.

Mya paused, the curtain parted to the outside, and her gaze lost its sheen of moonlight and turned black as the dark between the stars. "Yangoon. Dark things are happening in the south."

Then she stepped through the curtain and was gone.

"So you're not going to retire. That's a very good thing," Yamin danced and tumbled about.

Aung enjoyed the little puppet's happiness, and contemplated Mya's last words. Darkness in Yangoon where there were so many foreigners about. That could not be good.

Clouds gathered around Mount Popa's heights as Saya Lin pushed inside the curtains. "Well? What did the nat wife have to say?"

Aung sighed and stood, his knees surely creaking less than they had, which meant that Aung was going to have to live up to his end of the bargain—a bargain he would rather no one else knew about.

"Is it a secret, then?" Saya Lin asked, waiting.

Even with all his considerable powers as a composer of songs, Aung could not determine the best way to begin.

There was absolutely no way Saya Lin was going to be happy about going to Yangoon.

Join K.L. Abrahamson/Karen L. Abrahamson's Mystery Readers or Fantasy Readers!

If you'd like more of K.L. Abrahamson's mysteries, join other mystery enthusiasts and receive a free novel, a novella, and an award-nominated short story.

Or if your preference is fantasies, join other fantasy readers to receive three free novels.

To get your free books, go to

www.karenlabrahamson.com.

Don't go yet. Please leave a review!

If you enjoyed this book (and even if you didn't), it would be immensely helpful if you would leave a review at your favorite on-line retailer or on Goodreads (or both). Reviews help gain me visibility and they can bring my books to the attention of other readers who may enjoy them.

Thank you!

About this Book

I fell in love with the Burmese marionettes in 1997. I had been teaching English in Bangkok and had come across a wonderful little book called *The Illusion of Life* by Ma Thenagi, that gave the history and rules around the Burmese *yoke thei,* or 'small dolls'. Later that year, when I left Bangkok for Myanmar I vowed to research the puppets and made a point of visiting every show and marionette 'scholar' I heard about. In Mandalay I had the good fortune to meet a wonderful retired surgeon who loved the marionettes and had learned the dying art of carving them. He told me more about their history and their important role under the Burmese kings. I also had the opportunity to meet nat wives and to visit the wonder of Mount Popa. From these bits and pieces and from further research arose the antique Burmese world of the aging Singer, Aung Aung, and the impish Yamin. I hope their adventures bring you wonder and a smile.

About the Author

Karen L. Abrahamson is a well-traveled writer who has explored cultures and countries around the world but British Columbia, Canada, is her favorite place to come back to. She is the author of literary, mystery, romantic and fantasy fiction including the highly regarded Cartographer fantasy series. She lives on the west coast of Canada with killer whale, coyotes and eagles for neighbors.

When she isn't writing she can be found with a camera and backpack in fabulous locations around the world.

To find out more about her and her writing, visit
www.karenlabrahamson.com

Fantasy and Mystery by
Karen L. Abrahamson

Mystery (Writing as K.L. Abrahamson)
Through Dark Water

Fantasy Mystery
Aung and Yamin Series
Death By Effigy (Guardbridge Books)
A Death in Passing
Death In Umber

The Cartographer Universe
(in chronological order)
The Warden of Power
Impossible
The Cartographer's Daughter
The American Geological Survey Series:
Afterburn
Aftershock
Aftermath
Afterimage
Terra Incognita
Terra Infirma
Terra Nueva

Other Fantasy Novels
Ice Dragon
Emberstone
Mutable Things
The Crystal Courtesan

A Sneak Peak

Death In Umber: Book Three in the Aung and Yamin Mysteries

DEATH IN UMBER
A NOVELLA OF MARIONETTES, MAGIC AND MURDER IN HISTORIC MYANMAR
KAREN L. ABRAHAMSON

Chapter 1

The afternoon sun placed a heavy weight on Aung's shoulders, though his step was lighter than it might have been, for he carried only the weight of guilt instead of a physical burden. Under a cloudless blue sky he led the royal puppet troupe—keepers of the magical *yoke thei,* the eighteen-inch-tall Yamani-wood puppets—in a straggling procession along the narrow road past red-brick stupa, the twenty-foot-spires that dotted the dry plains like some kind of mushroom.

Occasionally he stepped off into dry grass or thorny ditches when one of the great, two-wheeled water wagons trundled past. The dun-colored oxen strained and sweated from the load of huge red urns filled with river water for the farms sprinkled amongst the stupa. The man-high wagon wheels and the puppet troupe's tired feet raised clouds of red dust that stained clothing and skin. Even the youngest apprentice, the singer Thura, had a red face creased with lines like an old man. The dust got into everything and tasted of mud and iron.

The road swung in a sharp curve around one of the mighty red brick *pahtos*—the temples that overshadowed the numerous smaller stupa. Indeed, many of the small spires sprouted as far as Aung could see across the red earth plain, for this was Pagan, the remains of a great kingdom that had—for some mysterious reason—vanished into history. What had once been a great civilization had left behind only this huge plain along the river, dotted with more spires and temples than anyone could count. Most were abandoned, but the largest of the temples were still used by the farmers and villagers who lived among them.

Perhaps they were the descendants of those who built this once-mighty place.

Aung stopped for a moment and looked back at the troupe. He alone of them was not burdened by one of the large wicker trunks that carried their precious *yoke thei* or the weight of the gong circle or the mighty carved dragon that carried the dragon drum. Even seventeen-year-old Thura was burdened by the pack of bamboo poles that would become the puppet stage and the wicker trunk that carried their curtains. And Saya Lin, their troupe leader, who had seen nearly the same sixty years as Aung, still carried the trunk of the Thagyar Min—the celestial king puppet.

The fact that Aung was not physically burdened was the greatest burden of all as he watched Saya Lin stumble and his friends struggle in the heat. But Aung was the eldest and over the past years his age had sapped his strength so that he no longer carried a burden—instead he had become a burden himself—or at least it felt so.

"Old friend, let me help you," Aung asked. "Let me carry your trunk for a time so that you can rest."

Saya Lin's tired gaze flashed up to him. "A puppeteer who cannot carry his puppet must retire. You know that as well as I. Now get out of my way."

Aung caught his arm. "Then perhaps we should rest for a while. Perhaps until evening. It will be cooler then."

Saya Lin ripped free and shoved past, no longer quite the old friend that Aung had known almost all his life. Aung stood there as the rest of the troupe shuffled past, leaving only Aung and faithful Thura beside him.

Aung and wiry-limbed Saya Lin had apprenticed together. They had become journeymen at their crafts— Saya Lin as a puppeteer and Aung as a singer. They had performed together over many years until they were masters of their arts and known and revered across all of Burma and perhaps beyond. But things had changed these past six months. The king still suffered their patronage, but for how long they didn't know. The murder of their Min puppet, the effigy of the human king, had left them a flawed troupe, and when the king got wind of it, he would surely withdraw his patronage. If he learned that they had been so flawed even during their recent royal performances—well, who could say what kind of revenge the king would wreak?

Now, after Aung's insistence had led them to a nearly disastrous visit to the home of the king of the nats, the spirits, he was insisting again. This time, at the request of the king of the spirits and against Saya Lin's wishes, Aung was leading them again, this time to the troubled south and the city of Yangoon.

"He is just tired, Master. It is a long, hot journey I had hoped not to take again," Thura said. He was so young, and straight-backed and with a voice so sweet, Aung had insisted he be his apprentice, even though the lad had been born to the Chin Hills people. He wore his blue *paso*—his sarong—with the front panel pulled up between his legs and tucked into his waistband to allow the air around his ankles. A vest and light cotton shirt protected his back and shoulders from the pack he carried.

Aung nodded. "He bears great burdens as our manager and leader. It is more than a puppeteer should have to carry, but someone had to assume that task."

He set out after the troupe with Thura at his heels, feeling the weight of the sun and of his decisions, for truly he was responsible for the growing schism between himself and Saya Lin.

After their escape from the king's palace in Amarapura, it was Aung who had insisted on visiting Mount Popa—to near fatal results for some of the troupe. He was also the one who had made a deal with the King of the Nats. In return for the mighty spirit king, Min Mahagiri, assuming some of Aung's burden of age, Aung would continue to seek ways to keep the old faith present in the people's lives and would solve the mysteries that clouded justice. The first task Min Mahagiri had set was to travel to Yangoon. Saya Lin had not been happy, for it was Saya Lin's job as leader to determine their travels and Yangoon was best avoided, for it was dangerous with too many foreigners about.

But Yangoon was many days' journey overland through country that would parch a man, so now they traveled to Pagan town in hopes of hiring a boat to take them down the length of the Ayeyarwady River.

Beside them, the huge dark bulk of a pahto grew up out of the earth like a boil upon the plain. Above the tops of the dusty htaung trees with their twisted branches, seven great tiers of brick lifted into the sky in a sullen pyramid, surmounted by a giant corncob-shaped pinnacle. On each step, three great vacant doorways yawned blackness into the day as if they screamed rage or pain or...

Aung didn't know. But this was a haunted place. The people who lived here might venture into such a place to pray at the ancient Buddha images, but it was not for him. Not, as far as he was concerned, for anyone living.

Ahead, the troupe seemed to avert their faces from the pahto. Aung did the same. Just let them get to the river, leave behind this haunted place and the ills that had befallen them. In the south, in Yangoon, surely it would not be as inhospitable. They would just need to be careful.

Just past the narrow, walled lane that led to the temple's walled courtyard, a thicket of htaung trees and thorn brush offered shade from the sun. Saya Lin threw off his burden with a groan and sank down onto the ground beside his trunk.

"It is too hot. We should rest here for the afternoon and continue our march in the cooler evening," he said.

"But that's what you..." Thura started.

Aung grabbed his arm to stop him. "He is our leader. It is up to him to decide."

The other troupe members settled their precious bundles to the earth and slumped down beside them. Thura and round-faced Zeya, the apprentice puppeteer, gathered kindling from under the trees and brought it to broad-shouldered Nyein, the dragon drummer. He lit a fire and readied a small pot to boil rice for a lunchtime meal.

It was a dusty place and Aung listened to the hoo-hoo, hoo-hoo of the ghostly gray doves and the wind fluting in the doors and windows of the darkened temple. As the moments ticked past, he felt the shadow of the huge structure creep across the dusty fallen walls and dry fields toward them. In the rainy season, this field would grow in the midst of all this desolation—he could see the furrows of last year's oxen-drawn plows crisscrossing the dirt—but now it was a desert of brown scrub grass between the lines of withered trees.

Soon the fire burned merrily and the pot of water steamed. Aung stood to ease his back and step beyond the huge structure's reach. His tired troupe mates talked quietly and dozed on the ground. Thura and Zeya had wandered farther down the road, apparently forgetting the trouble that had befallen them when they went exploring not so long ago. Aung glanced up at the omnipresent temple with its huge doorways and cracked and crumbling niches that might once have held something more.

Something moved in one of the doorways on the second tier of the temple.

Startled, he looked more closely. This was more than a bird. Surely he had seen something—a flash of umber?—in one of the doorways.

He stepped closer to the narrow road leading to the temple courtyard and the tall, carved lintels that guarded the entrance. Surely something stirred in that black maw of the main entrance and for a moment he thought of a tongue, unfolding swiftly enough to catch them and draw them in like some immense lizard.

He jerked back a step at the image, just as a pink-clad person stumbled out of the darkness. A shaven head gleamed in the sunlight. A nun, for only Buddhist nuns shaved their heads and wore the pink robes. She turned to the roadway and must have spotted Aung, for she raised her arm and called to him. Then she sank to her knees and collapsed face forward onto the ground.

Aung stood frozen. What had just happened?

"Did you see?" he asked, in case it was his imagination. In this strange place it was possible he had not seen what he thought. He turned to steady-headed

U Myint, who had come up beside him. U Myint had the high cheekbones of his Kachin grandfather's clan from near Myitkyina. He had the strong arms and shoulders of a puppeteer but his eyes were sad. His garuda puppet had been one of those lost in the debacle in Amarapura and he still mourned his small charge.

"A nun," U Myint said.

"She's collapsed," Aung called as he hurried toward her. Dust rose around his feet in a thick red cloud. A slight breeze swirled the dirt into his eyes and they were streaming by the time he knelt at the woman's side.

She lay face down in the dirt as if prostrating herself, her pink robes pulled around her, her small feet poking out from the hem, both shoulders bared where the fold of her robe had slipped when she fell. He hesitated to touch her, for it was not proper to touch a nun, but finally he caught her hand.

"Sister? Sister?"

He patted the back of her hand and her fingers shifted. She groaned and stirred in the dust and turned her face toward him.

Young. Very young, by the smooth skin of her thin face. Her eyes widened and she yanked her hand away and fumbled up to sitting, settling her robes across her shoulder again, just as Saya Lin and the others rushed to Aung's side.

Her dark gaze skittered from Aung to those behind him as she swayed and swallowed. Her face was thin, the skin almost translucent over bone as if she had not seen a full meal in a long while. Was that why she had collapsed?

"You." Her voice was soft and musical—someone Aung would like to hear sing. "You are them—the king's own puppet troupe."

Aung frowned and glanced back at Saya Lin. The old puppeteer stepped forward. "We are the Royal Yoke Thei."

"How did you know to come here?" she asked. Her voice had grown stronger even as her face grew puzzled.

"We are on our way from Mount Popa to the river," Aung said. "We are going to Yangoon." He heard Saya Lin stir behind him and knew his old friend's expression would have twisted.

She nodded. "I heard what happened at the festival. The pahtos and trees ring with the story the pilgrims tell of the puppeteers who solved a mystery and brought justice out of evil. Have you come to do the same here?"

There was an eager spark in the nun's dark gaze that sent a shiver of fear up Aung's back. What had they walked into?

He glanced up at Saya Lin again and watched the situation register in the hardening of Saya Lin's mouth.

"What has happened, Sister?" Aung asked just as Saya Lin said, "We are traveling through to the river."

The young nun looked from one to the other. "There is—trouble. Please help us."

She climbed to her feet, swayed a moment, but steadied. "Come, please." She turned toward the gaping entrance to the temple.

Aung hesitated, half-formed premonitions placing a light sweat upon his skin. Carved into the stone on either side of the door, where the effigy of the nat Min Mahagiri usually greeted visitors, lay ravaged places where someone had chiseled out the image. In anger? Doing the king's bidding to drive away the nats? The spirits of the land who brought good harvests and luck to homes had long been part of Burmese Buddhist beliefs, but the king had recently ordered the people to stop believing because he thought good karma would come to a country of purer Buddhism. The orders had led to a schism between the nats and those who listened to the king's orders. This defacing would anger the great nat, Min Mahagiri.

Aung shivered. This was—not a good place. At least not good for him. Farther along the stone wall were a series of beautifully carved Jataka stones that told the story of Buddha's life. At least that was right.

Sending a prayer to Buddha and to Min Mahagiri, he followed.

After the heat of the sun, stepping into the darkness was akin to diving into the deep pools of Inle Lake when he was a boy. Darkness enveloped him and, just as with the lake, glimmering shadows and secret streamers of light cut through the gloom to light a Buddha face in front of him and faded paintings on the wall. The scent of new incense filled his nose, and as his eyes adjusted, he made out a marigold-garlanded brazier set before a twenty-foot-high seated Buddha figure. To either side ran long, high-ceilinged corridors called ambulatories that ran the width of the building just inside the outer walls. The ambulatories would turn to continue on inside the square base of the huge temple.

The Buddha image was white-faced and serene, but the air around it seemed to quiver—in fear?

"This way," the nun hurried along the tall ambulatory that skirted the immense, inner mass of the pahto that would have been built to hold safe a holy relic of Buddha or another holy teacher. The curved ceiling towered above them, plaster still holding the remains of brilliant murals lost in the shadows. Their breath echoed as they followed after the swishing pink robes of the nun as she almost ran down the great avenue. Underfoot the stone was dusty and laced with footprints.

At the end of the ambulatory, where it turned down the next long side of the temple, the nun stepped to the outer wall and disappeared. When Aung arrived at the spot, he found a small stairwell had been constructed in a cunningly built fold in the wall. The stairwell drilled up through the brick until, high above, streamers of light lit the red stone as if from within.

Aung ducked into the tight space and trudged up the stairs, his troupe mates following. Up and up, his old legs protesting at the abuse as the stairwell turned and turned again. It was doubtful that he could have even made the climb if Min Mahagiri had not assumed the weight of some of Aung's long years. The passage was narrow enough that he scraped red dust onto his white shirt's shoulders before he reached the top where the stairs spat him out onto another platform. Another broad ambulatory stretched the length of this level of the temple. Shadows and whispers of the wind and something else slid through the shadowy ceilings, avoiding the light spilling into the hallway through the three open doors that illuminated more seated Buddha figures. They serenely surveyed the countryside. He'd seen someone move in one of those doorways.

The nun was halfway down the ambulatory and motioned back at him to follow as she steadied herself against the wall.

He hurried after her, down the long passage, with the wind cooled by the heights and the darkness so his sweat dried on his body. Another corner and the passage continued, more doors to the outside allowing in bright columns of light. More Buddha figures serenely peering out as if to bless the parched countryside. Here, Buddha's goodness had faded, but then Buddha was not a god, only a learned man. So the figures peered over the countryside providing guidance to those who lived in this parched place:

All is suffering. Everything passes away. Ergo, this suffering, too, will pass.

Aung could almost reassess his feelings about the place. Strange, yes. But grand. And sad, and comforting in a strange way. What a place it would have been when it was newly painted and in use.

Halfway down this length of the ambulatory in one of the dark places between the Buddha figures, another nun stood waiting.

The young nun panted up to her and together they faced Aung and the others. Then Aung realized that it was not just the two nuns he faced. There was a third figure, but this one was clad in umber robes and lay huddled like a sleeping dog up against the base of the ambulatory wall.

Aung went to his knees beside the curled form.

Young—very young. Really no more than a child. A novice monk, then, for he wore the umber robes of the monk in training just as Aung had done so many years ago. Sons were sent to study with local monasteries across Burma. The children learned to read and write and the Buddhist scriptures and monastic way of life before they were either released back to their parents or decided to continue with their studies. Most were young rascals who spent their time finding ways to break the monastery rules and were certainly never far from trouble.

This young lad had apparently found the ultimate trouble.

"He is dead," said the nun who had awaited their arrival.

Aung glanced up at her. She was old—much older than the nun who had led them here, though apparently not as spent as the young nun who still breathed heavily after her climb back into the temple. The elder nun's face was a skein of lines, her eyes two bright pebbles that caught the light, her mouth a crinkled maw of red from chewing betel. She had bony shoulders and arms twisted with old muscle. For all her apparent age, she stood straight-backed with no sign of infirmity.

"What happened?" Aung asked. Saya Lin nodded beside him.

The old nun shook her head. "I do not know," she said in a voice that creaked like stiff leather. "Saw Nang and I came to change the flowers today, just as we do every week. We found him here like this." She shook her head.

Saya Lin knelt beside Aung and together they leaned over the small curled form. His knees were bent as if he curled into himself. His small hands were claws as if he'd fought with someone. His mouth was open, as were his eyes. They had gone milky as if they looked beyond the darkness. Was he terrified as he awaited his next life? Had he made the passage to a better place or was he destined to become a hungry ghost?

Aung shook himself. This was a child. Perhaps this early death was penance for ill deeds in a past life. Something ill had been done to him to rebalance the karmic wheel.

"Look at his throat," Saya Lin murmured.

Time had allowed deep black bruises to form.

"Strangled, then," Aung said.

"But who would strangle a child?" Thura asked from among the other puppeteers.

Aung shook his head. "Who can say. It is an ill thing. An ill thing indeed."

He stood and gave Saya Lin a hand up. Both of their knees crackled and popped.

"Where is he from?" Aung asked. "They will need to be notified and the culprit found."

The two nuns looked at each other.

"But are you not the royal puppet troupe recently at Popa? We heard of you from pilgrims returning from the festival. Saw Nang spotted you on the road and I sent her to call you. I am Daw Ma Kyi, Abbess of our small community." She placed her palms together before her face and bowed to Aung.

He and Saya Lin copied her movements, for as abbess she was a learned woman, deserving of such deference.

"We dance the royal yoke thei," Saya Lin allowed, naming the famous royal puppets that were, unbeknownst to royals and commoners alike, also inhabited by magical nats, the remnants of the spirit of the great Yamani tree from which the puppets were carved.

Daw Ma Kyi looked from one to the other of the old men as if she was waiting. Then she looked beyond them to the others of the troupe. "I was told you investigated another death and brought the killer to justice. Is that not true?"

Aung cringed, for though he had revealed the true killer, it was the nats who brought the justice they thought the culprit deserved. It had not been pretty, and he had been troubled by his role in naming the killer. What if he'd been wrong?

He glanced at Saya Lin, whose expression had turned grim.

"The investigation was forced upon us when it affected the troupe," Aung finally ventured. "We are not investigators."

But the young body curled on the cold stone deserved better than this death. He should be rascaling through Pagan town. He should be laughing. Instead the cool breeze in the ambulatory was the only breath past his lips, the only sigh.

"We can at least help remove the body," Aung said. "He cannot stay here." He looked to Saya Lin, who finally nodded and then motioned to U Myint. U Myint had always been a steady, trustworthy fellow and since the loss of his garuda puppet he had worked hard to make himself useful. When other puppeteers might have become mired in despair at the loss of their "little brother," U Myint had kept his grief in check and assumed other tasks wherever he could.

"Bring the body," Saya Lin said.

Then he turned and left, the remaining puppet troupe members straggling after him. Aung and U Myint watched them leave, then turned back to Daw Ma Kyi and Saw Nang.

"Before we move him, let me look around a moment," said Aung. "This was where the boy was found? He was not moved?" He once more knelt beside the small body.

"We checked to see if he was alive, but otherwise we did not move him," Daw Ma Kyi said.

"Was he lying like he is now, or in some other position?" For the boy appeared to be huddled against the wall as if he'd cowered there. Or perhaps had been dropped?

He glanced up at the nuns.

"I think he was just like that," Saw Nang said. Daw Ma Kyi nodded.

Aung glanced at the bruises on the boy's neck and up at the wall. There were fresh scratch marks across the ancient paintings on the stone. Dropped, then. The killer had the young monk by the neck pressed against the wall and then dropped the body when the deed was done. The question was why.

The wind whispered answers as it dusted along the floor. He stood up, old joints creaking no matter that Min Mahagiri had relieved him of some of age's pain. He nodded at U Myint, who gently gathered up his small burden.

"We will help you take him to his monastery," Aung said.

The two nuns looked at each other again. "We have matters we must take care of here, first," Daw Ma Kyi said. "It is our fortune to provide incense and flowers to this temple's Buddha."

He noted then the two baskets abandoned farther down the tunnel and the faint perfume of marigolds in the air. "Then we will take the body down with us and pray that you join us when you have finished your task." He bowed and started back the way he'd come, U Myint following with the body.

Behind he heard the hushing sweep of the nun's robes against the stone and then their soft voices as they set about their business.

Through the broad arched doorways, the breeze carried the heat and dust of midday and for a moment

Aung regretted that he would be leaving the cool confines of the temple. At the corner he stepped into the stairwell, just as a shout of alarm came from outside. The premonition of disaster sent him stumbling down the stairs.

Look for *Death in Umber* at your favorite bookstore or online retailer, or go to www.karenlabrahamson.com.